RICHARD

THOMAS

STARING INTO THE ABYSS

This collection of stories is dedicated to everyone at The Cult, The Velvet, and LitReactor. You know who you are. I couldn't do this without your support. Also, a special thank you goes out to all of the editors, publications, and presses that supported these stories at Cemetery Dance, *ChiZine, PANK, Metazen, Murky Depths, Vain,* Dark Moon Books, *Nefarious Muse, Troubadour 21,* and *Colored Chalk.*

The following stories have appeared elsewhere, sometimes in slightly different formats:

"Steel-Toed Boots," "Committed," "Fallible," "Fringe," "Amazement," "Twenty-Dollar Bill," and "Honor" in *Colored Chalk*; "Maker of Flight" at *ChiZine* (Chiaroscuro), winner of the 2009 "Enter the World of *Filaria*" contest; "Freedom" and "Stephen King Ate My Brain" at *Nefarious Muse*; "Splintered" at *PANK*; "Stillness" in *Shivers VI* (Cemetery Dance); "Underground Wonder Bound" in *Vain* #5; "Victimized" in *Murky Depths* #15; "Interview" at *Troubadour 21*; "Ten Steps" at *ChiZine* (Chiaroscuro); "Twenty Reasons to Stay and One to Leave" at *Metazen*, nominated for a Pushcart Prize; "Transmogrify" in *Dark Moon Book Presents: Vampires* (Dark Moon Books); and "Rudy Jenkins Buries His Fears" in *Slices of Flesh* (Dark Moon Books).

KRAKEN PRESS

Published by Kraken Press 2013
www.krakenpress.com
Book design by George Cotronis
www.ravenkult.com

ISBN 978-91-979725-9-8

CONTENTS

MAKER OF FLIGHT

Moist damp air clung to his skin as he hunched over the workbench, goggles tight. Isaac held the little bird down with his gnarled hands, the incessant chirping pinging his ears.

"Schit schtill, wouldja," he said, as his mouth clenched shut, rotten gums pressed together tightly where teeth used to be. "Thish ish for your own good."

A flurry of blue wings batted at his knuckles, panic stretching the tiny bird's eyes wide, as Isaac poked around its backside with the silver screwdriver. Finding the latch, he inserted the tip into the screw and the cavity flew open, spilling sprockets and gears onto the scarred wooden surface. Quiet filled the room as he placed the still bird down. Wiping his brow and the top of his bald head, the candlelight bounced off the walls. Silence. Stretching his back, shoulders raised, he took a deep breath. Hacking out a deep, rattling cough he spat into a dirty handkerchief and stuffed it into his pocket. His dusty dungarees were more stain than fabric. The floor was lined with metal parts lurking in the shadows. Sheet metal and iron beams, mesh wire and rebar. Rust and mold drifted to his flat, wide nose, his sinuses raw from the turpentine and ether.

He reached across the desk, a hulking presence in the claustrophobic room. Grasping the tin cup, he swallowed the orange juice in one massive gulp, squinting his eyes shut for a moment of humanity. He'd paid a lot for this forbidden fruit. Scarce, yes. Gone? No. So many lies and rumors these days. But the sweet crank that was his only friend, nectar to the godless, she was his only reward for a job well done.

Dirt walls vibrated around him as another pod rambled up the shaft nearby. Soil spilled down on his glistening skull. His broad shoulders slumped over the bird to protect it. The tiniest fleck of earth dropped into its innards and he'd spend all day cleaning it out. So easy to jam up these fickle machines.

"4:21 ish a wittle earlwe today."

A gust of foul air eased across the room, and Isaac blinked, wrinkling his nose. The lone vent in his cell was of little help, content to belch rancid gas. A window, he thought. What I would give for a window. Blinking his eyes, the sunlight would probably blind him.

Standing up he walked over to the house of cards that was his shelves. Small glass jars littered the planks, cups and bowls of dented brass and tarnished tin. Screws, pins, springs. Gears, sprockets, filament, and rubber bands. His hand floated above the fourth shelf, faulty memory hunting down a replacement part for his little blue baby. They were all his children. Hundreds of them. Mostly Bluebirds, because that was what Diedre liked. But now and then he'd make a Cardinal anyway. Try to run it past his supervisor, his guard.

His only friend. Besides the juice. And the odd bits of moss that floated his way.

The moths were way beyond him.

"I'm coming darling, don't you fret," he muttered, glancing at the lifeless bird, tipped over on its side, guts spilled out in a pile of metal. Its vacant eyes still in shock, faded yellow beak open as if waiting for a worm.

"Ah, here it is," he said, his grubby fingers picking up a miniscule box and lens.

Back over to the desk he plopped down again, his hands a blur of efficiency, as he shoved one part inside another, screwed it in tight, every puzzle piece in the right place, every gear lined up, a latch set, and the compartment to its belly shut with a nearly inaudible click. Immediately the bird flapped its wings, scattering the dirty bolts and washers all over the floor. It chirped and chirped, flying in a circle, round and round, faster and faster. Isaac watched, a grin on his face. Eyes never leaving the bird he reached over and picked up a small box, entered a seven digit code, and punched the button. The bluebird fell from the air into his outstretched hand.

"It's ok. You'll be free schoon, darling."

On the far wall by the barely visible arc of a door sat a wicker basket. Shuffling over to it, he gently placed the bird inside, atop its inanimate brothers and sisters. Fifty-two birds in all. One dull red Cardinal buried in the mix. Daphne was her name, blue number fifty-two. They were all letter "D" today. Helped him keep his head straight. Daphne, Danube, Dominic, Delilah, Desiree, Davide.

"Not much room to schpare today," he said. But two over quota.

Standing next to the wood beam door, a pounding on the other side shook him out of his spell.

"Isaac, I'm coming in, sir," the voice squeaked.

He stepped back and eased into his chair, placing both hands on his meaty thighs, hands crossed as if waiting for a cup of tea, goggles misting as he freed his brood once again.

"Enter."

A tall thin boy poked his head in, dressed in rags, a dirty knit hat pulled tight over his head.

"Everything ok today Isaac?"

"Just peachy. Fifty-two."

"Excellent," the boy said, smiling as a muscle tic caused his left eye to flinch. Blinking. Blinking.

"Go ahead," Isaac said. "I'm ready."

The boy glanced down at the pile of birds, waiting to be taken. His eyes moved back to Isaac and in he crept. He grabbed the basket and stood up, arms full, that one moment of vulnerability that he dreaded each day.

"I'm going now Isaac."

"Be well, my friend," Isaac whispered, as the child disappeared behind the door. It pulled shut with a deep latching noise, locks turned and fastened, bolts passed and shut.

Looking down into his hand, Isaac stared at the tiny video camera, turning it over and over in awe.

"Wonder if da schky is schtill blue."

STEEL-TOED BOOTS

I tuck my long hair back up under the Caterpillar baseball hat. They don't like long hairs around here. I run my hands down my chest, buttoning up one more ivory disc on the red and tan flannel. Anything to help me blend in. Swinging my work boots out the driver's side of the dingy red Ford F-150, I lean down to tighten one lace. The Levi's complete the outfit, I mean what else could I wear?

It took me awhile to find this place. Up and down these back roads, these dirty trails took me on endless nights of bruises and deceit. I wasn't that big, but I could hold my liquor. Up to a point. I was able to avoid the fights by averting eye contact. And I was pretty generous with the beers. Most of the time it was pool, darts, and whatever game was on the tv. The blow jobs in the bathroom were just a bonus for me. They thought they were doing something awful, taboo. And while nobody really spoke up about Buddy's at the I-Hop or Denny's at three in the morning, scarfing down waffles and over-easy eggs, running with liquid gold over the toast and bacon, we all knew what went on here.

He never even looked at me. Maybe I wasn't man enough for him. I think he was what you call a bearchaser, he liked his men hairy, like a bear. It made sense. He didn't come here every night, he made his rounds to the sports bars and country shacks most of the time. But the urge would come over him, couple times a month, and I'd find him here at Buddy's. I wasn't going to hurt him. That wasn't what this was all about. I just wanted to understand.

Greeted by cigarette smoke, stale beer, and a hint of urine, I entered Buddy's for the third time in two months. I wasn't a regular yet, but the bartender was starting to know me.

"Hey Chris," he said, tossing the dirty hand towel over his shoulder, his own version of flannel rolled up at the sleeves, stretched taught across his ever expanding belly.

"What's up Randy," I said. "Beer me, bro."

"Bud?"

"Sure. Jack chaser, please." Please, I always said please, what the fuck was wrong with me. I can be such a pussy sometimes.

"Here you go, five bucks."

I grab the shot and down it, followed quickly by the beer. I place a twenty on the bar a bit louder then intended and turn to scan the room. For a gay bar it certainly didn't look like what I had expected. What that was, I don't know. Disco ball and day-glo paint? Half naked leather clad bikers and effeminate boys? After Brokeback I should've known better. They come in all shapes and sizes. Look at me, tall and skinny, porcelain hands and flawless skin. I had to stomp my hat in the dirt for hours, the same with the jeans. Perception you know.

He was playing pool. Didn't even see me, the same way it was at home. I'd blown a couple guys here, on the nights he didn't show up. There was this thing in the men's room, in the stalls. A glory hole they called it. Worked ok for me, and all I had to do was go in there and sit down. Didn't take long. Lots of horny guys in here, but none of them wanted to face the daylight of their hidden agenda.

Swallowing the beer, I needed a fresh round to steel my courage.

"Again Randy." I said, no please this time. I was learning.

He served them up and took his change out of the bills that were left. Down went the Jack, and I was off to the bathroom. Wood paneling held up scenic landscapes, and stuffed fish mingled with neon. Nothing much to speak of. But it had been home to me for awhile. It was the only time I got to really see my husband for who he was.

Sitting down in the second stall, beer in hand, tears trailing down my face, I waited for him. Maybe it would be tonight. Maybe he had finally noticed me.

It didn't take long for the hard cock to poke it's timid head through, and I stifled a grin as I went to work. It never took long. Part of my appeal was that I swallowed. But tonight I forgot to lock the door, and it would be my undoing.

He burst in with teeth bared, face flush with anger at his own weak actions. His fists were on my fragile cheekbones before I could say a word, the Budweiser shattering on the ground as he pummeled me into submission.

"Faggot, goddamn fucking queer," he grunted through his clenched yellow mouth. As I slumped to the ground his steel-toe boots connected with my stomach, over and over again.

"NO," I wheezed. "It isn't..."

"Shut up, shut the fuck up. I'm not gay."

STARING INTO THE ABYSS

I tried to protect myself, but he was too strong, my slender fingers too weak. The baby had been kicking on the way in tonight, excited to see his daddy maybe. But as I went under for the last time, my hat falling off, long blonde hair cascading from under it, our son stopped moving.

Too drunk to notice the little details, too full of crimson rage to notice the bra strap that was exposed, my husband stomped out of his gay bar hate crime, leaving us in a broken pile, blood seeping through my jeans, expanding at the crotch.

Two men entered the bar. Only one of us would leave it.

FREEDOM

The razor blade was getting rusty but he didn't mind. He paused for a moment and looked up at the small apartment and shook his head. What was the point.

The rancid kitchen was dark with gunmetal walls. Sunlight fought the pair of tall blinds to get through, a losing battle these days. The sink was piled high with dirty dishes. Dried-on enchiladas, cereal in bowls and pots with old noodles filled up the metal basins. The trashcan overflowed with empty pizza boxes, Chinese takeout and enough crushed beer cans to fill a homeless man's shopping cart. A large scarlet blown-glass ashtray shaped liked a daisy on acid perched on the countertop stuffed with cigarette butts. Old cans of cat food lay in the corner in varying stages of fossilization next to a filthy tin of water. A vintage fridge and stove in aqua were witness to the neglect.

The rest of the one bedroom apartment was coated in a film of dust and grime. The shower had enough rings to arouse a geologist. The toilet was a petri dish. In the living room a pile of old magazines were stacked on the hardwood floor. Wired. Playboy. Juxtapoz. Time. A lone Formica table held down the middle of the room, four chairs in cream leather and chrome. An obsolete Apple Macintosh Performa, a pile of melted candles and a whiff of patchouli sat atop it.

French doors with faded drapes in ivory lace led to a simple bedroom. A queen size mattress and boxspring sat with aplomb. A large tv with cigarette burns on the top sat on a thrift store bureau. Grey dust bunnies held congregation in a corner, the humble beginnings of an uprising at hand. A pile of dirty socks and underwear filled another corner, the smell of cat urine faint but distinct.

RICHARD THOMAS

Robert sat on the edge of his bed. Stubble clung to his face and he wore nothing but faded khaki shorts, frayed at the edges and dotted with drops of blood. At his feet a grey cat circled mewing for attention, rubbing his calves over and over again.

"I don't care, I don't care, I just don't care."

He pressed the razor blade into his left wrist and pulled it vertically up his arm. A tear ran down his face. He clenched his teeth while his arms trembled. A sigh escaped his lips. He closed his eyes and smiled for a second. A rivulet of crimson trickled down his forearm. He licked his lips and hunched his shoulders. He stared down at the blade contemplating Occam's Razor and the irony at hand. Flesh cried out for more abuse and he obliged it. A series of short cuts horizontal and not serious crossed his previous attempt. His chest rose and fell. His eyes were foggy and yet intently focused on the microcosm in his skin, every cell now screaming for a respite.

"...said it wasn't his fault. So I asked how wasn't it your fault? Your booze, your condom, your apartment. This is WCRP 106.9 Chicago. Real rock radio. A great day to be alive. Back after this."

"For a hole in your roof or a whole new roof...Fredric roofing..."

Robert slammed his fist onto the snooze button, silencing the clock radio on the nightstand, and sending a spray of blood flying. He placed the razor next to the clock and stared at the lattice work on his wrist.

"Just a little deeper."

He stood up and walked to the kitchen. His shoulder caught the corner, and he grunted as he entered off-balance. Opening the refrigerator there was nothing but a sad marriage of ketchup, mustard, pickles and beer. Lots of beer. Cases and cases. He grabbed a can of Budweiser, cracked it open and gulped half of it down in an instant. He studied the windows and sneered at the door. Leaning against the countertop he noticed a picture on the refrigerator.

He was six and his brother Bill was three. They stood in front of a huge oak tree that had been felled to build his house. His family's house. Two acres right behind his grandparent's two acres. His mother's mother. They were wearing some horrible combination of plaid pants, Garanimal t-shirts and second-hand sneakers. They had their arms around each other and squinted into the sun, smiles plastered on their faces, the pine scent of mosquito repellent in the air. The tree was nearly as thick as they were tall. The good old days. 1973.

The phone interrupted his reminiscence.
BRRRRRRRRRRRRRRRRRRRRRRRRRing.
BRRRRRRRRRRRRRRRRRRRRRRRRRRRing.
BRRRRRRRRRRRRRRRRRRRRRRRRRRRing.

"Hi, this is Robert. Please leave a message at the beep and I'll call you back as soon as I can. Thanks and have a great day. Peace."

"Hi Robert, this is Melissa with Artisan. We have an assignment starting tomorrow. It's mostly production, but some design. They'd prefer somebody with print experience, especially magazine and catalog work, so I thought of you. It's in the city and pays $28 an hour. Give me a call as soon as you get this. I think you'd be perfect. 312-845-6900. Melissa Dempsey. Artisan. Thanks! Bye." Click.

"You have 14 messages," said the monotone. Click.

Robert finished his beer and wiped his mouth with the back of his hand. Crushing the can he glared at the trashcan.

"Nothing but net," he said and took a short jump shot towards it. It landed on top of the pile and stuck the landing like an Olympic gymnast. He rubbed first his left bicep then the right and grimaced. He glanced at the countertop and the box of open razor blades. Several were scattered next to it, the rest still inside.

A rustle at the apartment door caught his attention. The metal flap of the mail slot lifted. In flopped the mail as it closed with a clank. Robert sighed and walked to the small pile of distractions. Six pieces: the ComEd gas bill for $48.56; a solicitation from the Salvation Army to renew his membership; a postcard showing the Space Needle at the 1962 Seattle World's Fair; an invitation to see DJ Dominatrix at Club PVC with two complimentary passes; a credit card bill for $124.56. He picked them up and placed them gently in a small wicker basket on a bookshelf by the door. Running his fingers over the books, dust fell while he traced a trail down the spines. Hemingway. Vonnegut. Tolkien. Kesey. Burroughs.

"YOU'VE GOTMAIL," the computer shouted from behind him. Robert walked over to it and pushed aside a stack of manuscripts in various stages of editing. He double-clicked the mouse and his AOL account opened up. 286 new messages. The latest was from his brother.

Robert,

Hey bro, where have you been? I've left you a couple of messages, but no response. Is this account still working? You never answered my last email either. Hope everything is OK. Fuck Laura, I never liked her anyway. Here's something funny for you. Call me.

JOKEOFTHEDAY: One day Superman was flying along, feeling kind of horny. He had a busy day ahead of him, but just had to satisfy his urge.

So he decided he would fly over to Wonder Woman's house to see what she was doing. As he got closer he used his x-ray vision, and to his surprise, Wonder Woman was lying on her bed totally nude.

Superman thought "This is great! I'll just zip right in there, do my business, and before she knows it, I'll be gone." So, Superman blasts in, right on top of Wonder Woman, does the deed at light speed, and is gone in a flash. Wonder Woman, not quite knowing what hit her says "WHOA! What was that?" and the Invisible Man replied. "I don't know, but my ass sure is sore!"

Robert smiled and headed back to the bedroom. He plopped back down on the bed and picked up the razor. He pressed it against the bulging vein in his forearm and dragged it towards himself, all the way to his elbow. A thin line of blood revealed itself, the flesh parting ever so slightly. The release.

A pounding on the door.

"Sergei, open up. Sergei. Open the fucking door," a female voice shouted. Robert paused, and stared in that direction. Quiet. Then the pounding continued.

"Sergei I know you're in there, open up."

"Go away," he hissed.

"Please Sergei. It's Tasha. It's important."

"Fuck." Robert put the blade on the nightstand, got up and shuffled to the noise. He unlocked the deadbolt as blood trickled down his forearm in tiny rivers dripping off his fingertips. He opened the door.

"Do I look like a Sergei?"

A statuesque brunette stared open-mouthed. Her ring laden fist stopped in mid-air. She was clad in a black tube top stretched to its limits, magenta hot pants and knee high leather boots painted on slender legs. A black leather purse hung from her hand.

"Damn."

"Where is Sergei?"

"I don't know any Sergei."

"What?"

"I don't KNOW any Sergei."

"And you are not Sergei?"

"For Christ's sake. Third base."

"What? I don't understand. I am Tasha. I only get here last week."

"From where Tasha?"

"Soviet Republic. I am student."

"Right."

"Are you OK? You are bleeding."

"I know."

Tasha looked down at the blood dripping off Robert's fingertips and then back to his face. She paused.

"You have beautiful eyes mister. But you are a mess."

"I am a mess."

"Can Tasha help you clean up?"

"Right. I don't think so." Robert closed the door on her eager face. But before it could shut, her hand shot out and stopped it with a speed and strength that startled him

"Please. It is OK. It is what I do. I am your new best friend."

"Really."

"Seriously. You have no interest in Tasha? You may be on your way to another place, but your eyes have time to drink me in." One hand on the door and the other on her hip, Tasha smiled, her dark eyes twinkling, her smile a pleasant change.

"Sure. Fuck it. Why not. Come on in. There's some Stoli in the freezer."

Tasha walked in smelling of whiskey, cigarettes and musk. She looked around. "Tsk, tsk. You've been a bad boy, mister. Let Tasha take care of you. I have three brothers back in Moscow. I know this mess when I see it."

"Tasha, I'm fine. But if you're pouring, pour two."

Tasha sauntered to the kitchen her sculpted ass begging for eyes as it swayed from side to side. It was not denied. The freezer door opened, and the sound of glasses clinking followed. She opened her purse and held it below the counter as she swept the box of razor blades into it. None were missed. She picked up the drinks and headed back into the living room.

"Come, we will sit and talk."

They eased past the French doors and sat on the edge of the bed. Leaning over she put the shot glasses down and then the bottle, her back to Robert. She opened the drawer and swept the blade into it. A twist of the cap and the shots were poured.

"Come closer Robert. Closer, I won't bite. Drink with me."

"How do you know my name? I didn't tell you it."

"Oh Robert, in Soviet Union we must think on our foot every day. Your mail says Robert, that pile on the shelf, the table, the counter. The place just screams Robert. Come sit."

"OK."

Sitting on the edge of the mattress next to Tasha his shoulders dropped. She handed him a shot.

"Nazdarovya," she said raising her glass and they downed the vodka. "Stay put."

Tasha got up and clomped to the kitchen.

The sound of running water was followed by tearing paper and she returned. Tasha picked up Robert's left arm and blotted the wet paper towel up and down it. His face tightened as he sucked in air. And then he relaxed. The blood disappeared leaving thin white lines filled with pink. The silence was deafening as she cleaned his wounds. The towels got darker by the minute. Robert's eyes closed and tears pushed out from beneath them. Tasha leaned over and kissed his wrist leaving the same crimson in fleshy lips.

"If you want pain, I give you pain. If you want release, I give you release. If you want death, I can't do that. Enough Robert. Whoever she is, she is not worth this. We have a saying in former Soviet Union. Women are like bus. Another will be along in three hours." She grinned a sly grin and pulled his head to her ample bosom. Robert went slack, and sighed into her chest. Baby powder and vanilla masked the powerful thumping of her heart. Tasha turned off the lone lamp and the bedroom plunged into darkness.

Down in the alley Bill sat in his green Ford Explorer staring at the dark bedroom window. The city wrapped around him like a soiled blanket. Garbage trucks loaded the waste of another week gone by – milk going sour, dirty diapers fermenting. Car horns blared and middle fingers were raised as smoky exhaust and burnt oil mingled . The bass of hip-hop thumped by on vibrating wings paired with skunky weed and two-bit cigars.

"Best $500 I ever spent."

COMMITTED

I keep falling down.

Grey clouds fight the dark sky. The worn treads of my sore feet pound the sidewalk, every gum wrapper and empty beer can screaming for rain. Get inside, you idiot, they yell. Shut up. One more voice I don't need.

Stupid fucking shoes, these goddamn ragged old boots. The laces come untied no matter how many times I loop them around my ankles. Denim is no match for concrete. And neither is flesh. Red sticky patches leak from my knees to match the ones on my knuckles.

Sweat peppers my forehead, and the stench under my leather jacket is getting rank, even for me. I reek of rotten cheese left out in the sun, a whiff of roadkill flattened to a stain.

But I finished that goddamn God of War, I'll tell you that much. Fucking Playstation. Nobody can tell me that I don't finish things, that I'm a total loser. She spit on me, for Christ's sake. Then I back-handed her across the room. That shut her up. Eventually, for good.

The weight in my back pocket tugs at my jeans, one more fucking irritation. At least it warmed up. Snow flurries last week. Then cool breezes and dodgy sun today. What the fuck. I forget my jacket, and freeze. I wear layers and sweat my ass off.

At the end of the day it wasn't so much that I hated my boss, David Fucking Hernandez, as I just needed to smack his head with the broad side of the shovel. Another voice quieted. Thank God. The list is getting smaller. No more gravel and tar for me, no sir. No more backbreaking, mind numbing work.

I shift the gun to my inside jacket pocket. It is almost as annoying, but at least when I did a facial, my pants wouldn't pool around my ankles. I pull the last Budweiser out of my outside pocket and twist off the cap, the metal clinking to the sidewalk at my feet like angry tin tear drops. 24 beers, 23 gone. Another accomplishment. It had seemed insurmountable last night, but here I am, on top again. Finished. Two cigarettes left, I know that much.

"Hey buddy, no open containers," the guy outside Kinko's says, his little blue nametag shouting Ray, I'm a fag, I'm a doormat, I don't eat pussy, and I smoke Marlboro Lights, come make a copy, be my friend.

"Fuck off asshole, and mind your own business," I say, slow-ing down to eyeball him, gulping down the rest of the red label that had been my only friend last night. I cock back my arm and fling it at his head, sailing it high and wide, shattering off the brick wall.

"Jesus Christ," he mumbles as he hunches over. "I'm calling the cops, fuckwad."

"Do that, my friend, and it'll be the last thing you ever do."

He scuttles back inside, glancing over his shoulder. It doesn't matter. He can call the fucking cops. It'll be too late. Heather. David. And one last stop at the post office. Up ahead I can see the stream of ants going in and out of the doors. In this way, out that. Packages here, stamps over there. Bladdity blah, and bippity bip. No more. It wasn't enough having a conversation with Gary, the postman. They just replaced him. And the mail keeps coming, all of it, keeps on coming. It never stops. Well I say enough.

I stop to check the cylinder. Six. Five for them and one for me. No more credit cards bills, no more red lined utility notices, no more catalogs of porn, no more church bulletins, no more anything. I grab the door and hold it open for a smiling blonde in tight jeans, the little whore. She was somebody's daughter, true, but she was also somebody's blowjob queen, somebody's incompetent waitress. No ice I said, Dijon mustard I asked, sugar for my motherfucking iced tea, please, I asked. No, she was no ray of sunshine.

In I go.

SPLINTERED

[1]

At night, when I finally fall asleep, exhausted with stress, scenes unfurl in black and white. I see her hand on his knee at the dinner party, laughing. I don't miss the smirk that slips across her face as she closes the door on her way out of the apartment. She hums a tune while washing dishes, and I have no idea what it is. Her answers are the same: nothing, nobody.

Floating in the room, the shadows hug the muted walls of our apartment, the heavy moon a flash of blindness whenever the hot breath of the clinking heater pushes the drapes apart. My eyes are clamped shut against it all. But maybe that's the idea. Turning away from it all. Trying not to look at what is right in front of me. Her laughter in the hallway, away from me, her eyes darting to the corners of every room, pushing her autumn tresses back behind her ears. She makes time for me, we hold hands at the dinner table, chewing the pasta, downing the thick wine. She comes to me in the night, the darkness, her arms wrapping around me, pulling me to her, under, and in. She makes me weak.

IF YOU DECIDE TO GO TO WORK, proceed to [4]

IF YOU DECIDE TO STAY HOME, keep reading.

[2]

I feign a sickness. The more she wants me out of the house, her eyes squinting, hand on her hip, cocked, eyes ablaze, the worse I get. I vomit into the toilet out of spite. She avoids me, her phone buzzing on the kitchen table, nicking the faded wood, dancing next to the plate of dried yellow egg yolks, remnants of toast, lipstick kiss on the white porcelain cup. I barely hear her when she leaves.

"I'm going out, be back later."

The door slams shut before I can get off the bed. No offer to stop by the drug store, no Tums, no Pepto-Bismol, no run to the grocery for chamomile tea, wildflower honey. There is no sweetness in this departure. It is panic.

Anger. Maybe I'm already dead.

    IF YOU DECIDE TO SLEEP, proceed to [4]

    IF YOU DECIDE TO FOLLOW HER, keep reading.

[3]

I pull on battered jeans, and a soft, grey t-shirt that she's tossed over the back of the kitchen chair. It was mine, it had been, now it is hers, or maybe not. Discarded. Maybe it is mine again. A black sweatshirt over that, and then a leather coat, my boots tugged on, and I'm tipping over, leaning towards the sharp edge of the bureau, struggling to keep my balance, the corner calling to my eye, begging it to gouge itself out, knowing that it has seen enough.

Outside, the taxi is pulling away, two heads close together. I chase it down. It slows at the corner, and turns right. I dash across the parking lot, a sharp pain in my side, cutting it off, and it veers to the left. Darting across the traffic, the northbound bus belches smoke. I slap it on the ass, eating its exhaust. Across the street, the blur of yellow comes to a halt at the stop sign trembling in the wind. I accelerate, heat rushing over my ribcage, a trapped bird banging around inside, pecking at the muscle, wanting to escape. A wink of green, and it turns right, as I sprint across the lawn, jumping over the low-slung cast iron, my boot catching, and I'm reaching out in front of the cab, lights rushing over me as my knees hit the road, tearing through the denim, tires screaming. In my head, I'm screaming. Back in our apartment, I'm pulling her hair from behind, flesh against flesh, her neck bared to me, lips curled back, eyes glassy, and she's screaming, "Yes."

Metal on my arm, my chest, pressure, splitting, a heavy weight settling on my legs. Car doors open, footsteps.

There is a bell jingling, I'm getting my wings, a door bangs against a wall, light spilling over me from the supermercado, voices. Something shatters on the sidewalk, small circles of orange roll under the cab, my eyes open, boots, voices, a radio cackles. There is a hand on my neck, fingers, ohmygod, the smell of menthol, lemons.

She is whispering in my ear. Right back, I said.

IF YOU DECIDE TO END YOUR STUPIDITY, stop here.

[4]

There was very little sleep last night, her sandalwood perfume drifting to me, the indentation on her bare shoulder not quite teeth marks. I'm not sure when she came in. Somehow I'd made myself sick, really sick, a fever running across my forehead, my feeble pale body drenched in sweat. I had been wrapped in panic, betrayal a hammer pushing nails into my temples, while I tried to find air to breathe.

Leaving her at the kitchen table in nothing but a t-shirt, an old grey v-neck of mine, her cleavage disappearing into the soft fabric, her fingers tapping on the table, I can hardly do it. I open my mouth to speak, and snap it shut. It's all been said before. She looks up, eyes like saucers, then away to the window. The bare tree branches are like arthritic fingers, skeletal, aching.

I'm a trusting soul, it's in my nature, so I can't believe it. I'm the nice guy, no motorcycle, no tattoos, no drinking problem. She'll have to rub it in my face.

I'm dead to the world, riding the subway into the city, bodies bumping against me, jostling my thoughts. My eyes are rimmed with blood, so I hide behind tinted lenses, drifting off again.

When I round the corner of the cube farm, to my cubicle of grey, the phone is already ringing, so I snatch it up.

"Hello?"

"Sorry, wrong number," she says.

The voice says. The woman. A gasp of breath, her hand reaching up to cover her mouth, his lips on the small of her back. Why the call? She wants me to know. She wants me to leave, to confront her. She can't do it on her own.

IF YOU DECIDE TO BE A MAN, go to [6].

IF YOU DECIDE TO LIVE IN DENIAL, keep reading.

[5]

The day is nothing but an echo. It is eternity, and it is one long exhale. Back into the cold, car horns, a filmstrip running by, a key inserted, and the cage opens. The kitchen table has become a turnstile. It is where we come and go. I sit. The glass is full, and then it is empty. Amber reflects the light, and then warms my gut. I stare at the door, until it slips away, blurs into a cornfield, husks slapping at my face, the leaves nipping at my bare arms, dusk sliding over the sky, gunmetal turning into the bruises left behind.

"Honey, honey…"

I sit up. The apartment is dark now, a rustling from the bedroom. I stumble towards the sounds. Drawers are opening, hangers clanging, a silhouette passing in front of the windows, and then nothing. Silence.

I click on the bedside lamp, and she lies on the bed naked. I click on the bedside lamp, and the room is empty.

I click on the bedside lamp to an empty dresser, unhinged.

I click on the bedside lamp, and she stands still, caught.

I click,

I don't.

She isn't here. She never really was.

IF YOU DECIDE TO END THIS MISERY, just stop.

[6]

I don't give her the chance. I strike first. I have four pairs of jeans, three flannels, six Polo's, one pair of tennis shoes, twelve balled up pairs of socks, a cigar box full of cash, a pack of condoms. No underwear. No books. No hesitation. I stuff it all in an old leather bag, a doctor's bag that my grandfather left me. I piss on the bed, the thread count no longer an issue. I stomp on her vinyl records, turning them into splinters. I take her photo albums, dump them in the bathtub, douse them in lighter fluid, and drop a match on top. I take a pair of scissors and cut out the crotch of every pair of her panties.

I leave my keys on the kitchen table.

IF YOU DECIDE TO STOP BEING A DOORMAT, keep on walking.

FALLIBLE

I retch into the stained porcelain until my stomach is a twisted knot. Empty now, there is nothing but gasping air, a sheen of sweat coating my forehead.

I used to lie awake at night and fantasize about such things. Romanticize these horrible moments and how I would react. War, rape, fistfights. Violence layered upon violence, a momentary release of every thread of anger that had knitted its way through my being.

It doesn't work that way. In the end I was less than a man.

Their screams are what I hear, every night, and a drift of smoke is all it takes to set me off. I've told my neighbors to stop. That it's against the law now. They laugh, and scratch at the track marks on their arms. It ain't the Four Seasons, they cackle.

I don't know what would be easier, or more rewarding, I wonder, as I hold the cold metal in my hand, and spin the chamber around. Wrapping my mouth around the barrel and pulling, or making that trek next door to take them out first. It spins, ratcheting around and around. I've pulled it twice tonight. The hollow click a tiny echo in my empty hovel at the end of my rope.

I had a job once. It mattered. Once.

Cigarette smoke drifts under my door, and as I shut my eyes, tears squeeze out, and I mutter the endless mantra that I repeat five hundred times a day.

"Forgive me Lord. Please, forgive me."

I can't sleep any more. And no matter how many cases of beer I put down, how many times I run a razor over my wrists, I am still numb to the core, and yet am in so much pain that every pore of my body screams out for reprise. I am autistic with loss.

It was my cigarette. I fell asleep. It was the heat at first, but the smoke that really woke me. Choking and gagging, I rolled off of the couch into the darkness. The crackling was deafening, except for their screams. Those I could hear. Flashes of red and orange, hypnotic in its intrusion. The front door fell in under heavy boots, and beacons of failing light. My eyes stung, and I could not see. As I passed out, their voices pierced my eardrums. His, and hers.

"Daddy...daddy. HELP. Daddy."

STILLNESS

Darkness spilled over the land. Ten locks were fastened, turned, and keyed as fast as his ruddy hands could move. If you fell asleep with the pale sunshine drifting down on your face, you could wake up in a room full of strange men with a gun in your mouth . He shook the door handle several times, satisfied that it was indeed locked.

Out of breath, his chest heaved, brow coated with sweat. Michael flicked off the lights and squatted in the corner. A lone red dot flashed across the room, his only link to the outside world. Another night of cold corned beef hash right out of the can. Unprepared, again. It would be his demise.

He crawled to the one open window, floor to ceiling, a towering presence. He had to move as if a ghost. He had to close the thick metal shutters without drawing any attention. He eased up to them and with all the patience he could muster, pushed them closed, meeting with a familiar clink. Silence.

"So how was your day, honey?" he asked the tiny, dim apartment.

"Great Michael, and yours?"

"Same old same old. Spent four hours remote gassing the vehicles. Posted to my blog. Had a can of Minestrone soup. Lite, because I'm watching my cholesterol. And then I fell asleep on the mattress covered in a blanket of dust, bed bugs, and an odd stain or two."

"I'm sorry baby. Do you miss me?"

"Every day, Missy. Every goddamn day."

Michael buried his face in shaking hands while his body was wracked with grief. Two years. Not a single solitary voice or face in two years. But his role was essential. Leave, and the swarms would come. The masses would flock. The herds would migrate, and all would be lost.

He crawled over to the ancient computer monitor that sat on the floor, its beacon a dull bleed from this scab of a life. It was time. He punched the enter button, and out the tiny slots in the metal shutters he saw flames shoot high into the sky. Brilliant yellow masked with velvet and rust. The screeches came next, crackling and bellowing, as the frames fell from the sky, the musculature tipping over with a dull thud. He shoved his fingers in his ears while he rocked back and forth, empty inside, with little reason to care.

Shirtless, his thin frame toned and tan, Michael shoveled the dead creatures into the fire pit. He glanced up and down the wall, as he did every morning, watching it extend as far as his eyes could track. To the horizon in every direction. Nothing new today, but he had to look. It was his only television. This one opening, the one gap, was his to maintain. It was his trap to set, and it worked like a charm. In the pit, the long thin bones of the airborne creatures mingled with the massive limbs of their masters. And others.

Leaning the massive shovel against the stone wall, he limped to the far side of the courtyard to wrestle the chicken fat over. Giant tubs of oil, grease, fat and other waste. Tubs, cans, buckets, whatever he could find. It still remained, scattered all over the city. Leftovers from every abandoned McDonald's, Burger King, and Kentucky Fried Chicken. Especially the KFC. He grabbed an old milk carton, twisted off the top, and poured it over the towering pile of bone and sinew. Around and around the pit he walked, dousing it in the rotting liquid. When he was done, he tossed the carton on the pile and stood back. Let it sink in before lighting it on fire.

Decisions today. Into town, or stay here. Canned food, or a nap. The heavy gun at his hip said nap, but his boredom and hope said town. As he strolled past the rotting pile, a crimson claw shot out of it, clasping down on his thigh.

The pistol was out of its sheath before the claw could sever his limb, and he shattered the exoskeleton into a thousand pieces with a single shot. Sometimes they didn't go down easy. Eyeing the opening to the vast desert that lay before him, he blinked several times, and then gently placed his hands on the tear in his leg. The faded Levis had been no match, and the parting of his flesh oozed fresh blood over the fabric.

"Okay, staying here today. Time to play medic."

Ambling back inside, now limping with both legs, Michael pulled a pack of matches out of his pocket and bent one back. Striking it across the cover it burst into flame and ignited the rest of the pack.

He tossed it onto the scrap heap and went inside. A dull whoomp ran around the base of the bones and up the pyramid of flesh. The smell made his stomach growl, against all will and hope.

There was only so much automation could accomplish. He had to be here. But why the journey across the valley of death couldn't be made, he didn't know. So little communication, and what he got was difficult to decipher. His family was long gone. Missy, and his son, Mike Jr. Mikey. Mikey Mouse. Junior. The little man. He didn't let himself revisit those days very often. His son, not at all. It was too much. So he held his station, and did his job. His service had been up three months ago, but nothing had come across the transom. He wouldn't know where to go if he did take off. What direction, how far it would be, where they were. He'd been in the dark since the beginning.

Michael lay on the same rotting mattress as yesterday. The door was locked. The shutters were closed. He sat up and reached across to the computer to push the button.

Enter.

Shrieks. Bellows.

He lay back in the dark, and contemplated his options. He gazed over at the medication on the floor, the pile of empty plastic containers. No more.

The days passed as they always did. Piles of bones, and the endless beatdown of the hot summer sun. Nights were filled with nothing but the pulsing of his heart, and the crackling of bodies burning down into a pile of ashes.

Until they came.

He thought they were coming to save him.

A loud chopping noise outside his apartment jolted Michael out of his sleep. Running to the window, he pressed his eye up against the slot, and was rewarded with a glimpse of a low flying helicopter. Sections of light panned across the courtyard, voices in the night, lost in the whir of blades slicing the air.

They were here. Finally. He could leave.

Running to the door, he clicked open the lone lock. A phone in the kitchen rang, a startling jingle out of the void.

Rushing out into the hallway he left behind several things. A pile of mail pushed to one side of the door, almost three feet high. An overflowing garbage can in the living room, filled with empty Chinese takeout, fast food bags, and pizza boxes. A fully furnished apartment, complete with brown leather sectional, four-post king size bed, and plasma TV bolted to the wall. And a small wooden table covered with prescriptions, some empty, some spilling onto the table. But the ones with the most recent dates were full and unopened.

Down the stairs he flew, as voices and radios crackled all around. Boots crushed in the front door, the thin frame splintering as he ran out the back.

"They're here. I can go home," he said, lips moving in a barely audible mumble.

Into the courtyard of the apartment building he flew. A row of bushes almost ten feet high ran to both sides, with a gap in the middle, chain link fence wide open. Three Weber grills sat next to each other, covered in gasoline, charcoal and greasy black soot. To one side a circle of rocks formed a makeshift fire pit, filled with bones of all sizes. Tiny bones the size of cats and dogs. Larger bones, a femur, a foot, the size of a small child. And even bigger still, the skulls of adults, tibias and jawbones. Bits of fabric, denim and leather mixed with the melted down stubs of shoes, boots, and purses.

He stared at the mess, the stench of burnt flesh overwhelming. Sweet and meaty, the sour tang of rotting underneath. Side to side he glanced as the light poured back and forth over him. A garbled mess of squawking and rotor blades as the wind whipped around him. Bits of cement and ash swirled, striking him in the face and arms. Looking down he was only clad in a dingy pair of what had once been white underwear, his arms and legs covered in scrapes. He looked up to the gap between the hedges as the stormtroopers poured through, guns raised, masks and helmets tight. They were on him like a swarm. A herd of beasts.

FRINGE

Holding the bloody microchip in my hand, my jaw hung open as a wave of disbelief washed over me. With my free hand I grasp for the cold beer sitting on the Formica table and knock it over, sending it clattering to the beaten grey tile beneath. My eyes can't leave the chip, though. The tiny yellow light pulses amidst strands of hair, and a piece of what must have been my flesh. The trickle at the back of my head feels like a river, as the room swims, and I fight for my vision, grasping at my straw consciousness with slippery fingers. There is a pounding at the door. I can't move. It is coming back to me, little by little.

Tuesday, the delivery guy. Pizza that I know I didn't order. The driver standing there, just a little too old, his shoes a little too nice, and square. Something too slick. His eyes too sharp.

Wednesday the pile of boxes outside my door. UPS. Not for me. But they made it inside. Moments later the pizza guy's twin brother stood there, apologizing for the mistake. But I hadn't even called them yet. He glanced around the room as he wheeled them out. Earpiece.

Thursday, a cop pulled me over. I wasn't speeding. I wasn't doing anything wrong. But he knew my name before my license was in his hand. A sparkling white grin plastered on his face.

Now it was Saturday. And as I glance across the room at the glowing computer monitor, the cursor dances a jig, clicking around my desktop, starting up applications, scrolling down menu bars, pulling up histories: How to make your own bomb with household products. What exactly IS anthrax? Assassinating a president: 10 tips for success. What bothers me most is the lettering on the microchip. It's Russian. I think. It certainly isn't English.

RICHARD THOMAS

It had started as a joke. Something to do on a slow night besides study. There were groups on campus, attendance sheets to sign, rallies to attend, skirts to chase, beers to drink.

The screech when I answered my cell this morning had been that of a fax. I think. It didn't sound quite right for a fax. Glancing up at the dark windows across the courtyard, the other apartments were dark. All but one. A man stood there, with something in his hands. A red dot bounced around the kitchen. A singular image from my cell phone flashed across my eyes. A man walking a dog, older, with white hair, leaning over to kiss a tight little blonde. Not his daughter, that was for sure. Their heads spun around. Familiar. One quick email to a couple hundred people. Look at this guy. Caught in the act. How funny is that?

The pounding continues at my apartment door. Unable to move, I can only stare at the weak frame as it shakes and splinters, dust breaking free, tiny microbes spilling into the space.

Nobody ever takes me seriously. Sure, I wear all black. Sure, my head is shaved. The swastika is a good luck charm of the early aviators. The fertilizer is for my garden. I grow roses. And I've had that rifle for a long time, for hunting. I'd only recently run out of ammunition. This was a mistake. My head grows heavy and thuds to the table, the tiny chip clattering to the floor. My limbs twitch as the darkness swallows me whole.

The high whine of a fast moving object, the tinkling of glass, and a tiny pfft of dust from the drywall. There is a crack at the door, voices and footsteps, and hands at my shoulders. "Comrade," he whispers.

Or is it Conrad.

UNDERGROUND WONDER BOUND

The massive tower of black muscle looms alone in the alley, the only sign of life as far as the eyes can strain. A solitary light bulb descends from above him, his neck twisting back and forth, scanning for movement.

"Marcus, what's up bro. Keeping you busy?"

Nothing. Stoic. Leather clad ironman, battered jeans over tree stump boots.

"Oh. Right. My bad."

Turning to my companion, the newly blonde and tightly wrapped Veronika, I bare white teeth, sharpened incisors flashing for a moment.

"No worries babe, just gotta get the word of the day. Hold on."

I pull my wafer slim cell phone out of my black suit coat, and flip it open. 8 messages. Scanning, scanning, looking for the key. Skipping stock quotes, skipping Liz from last week, skipping the White Sox final score, skipping Brian's whiny message no doubt, ah, here it is. Thursday. The word.

She stands before me with a glimmer in her mossy eyes. A dull glaze coats them as dark mascara and grey shadows submerge her gaze deep into her murky center. As always, I'm halted in my actions by the breathtaking form she inhabits, the muscles that seem to flex even when she is standing still. Thighs ripple as she shifts her weight from one high heel to the other. A plump ass mocks me atop forever legs, a tiny waist begs me to lift her with one arm to my pounding chest. I often have to look away, her lips dewy, on the verge of trembling. The stench of rotting milk snaps me out of her distraction, back to the task at hand, away from the tiny black dress and delayed gratification.

"Everything okay?" she asks.

"It's all good. We're set."

"Marcus, sorry, I know the rules. Apocalypse, my friend."

He stands aside, revealing a rusty metal door, hexagonal bolts framing its edge.

"Have a good time, Jacob. Always nice to see you," he grunts, the baritone rumbling through the quiet brick walls and stained concrete."

We enter the dim hallway, recessed lights glowing red in the walls. She reaches down and grabs a hold of my hand, her tiny thin fingers more powerful then they look.

"Hey, it's cool you know, we don't have to come here tonight."

"I don't want to waste the coke, baby. You know how it makes me feel."

"Sure. I hear you. I just wanted you to know that it'd be no big deal if we backed out."

"I'm good Jake. After that hunk of muscle at the door, I'm a little moist already."

There is no sound down the hall but our shoes drifting over the carpet, and the distant bass of music in the distance. At the bend in the hall, a sharp turn left, stands another massive doorman, arms crossed in defiance. A tiny ledge holds a tall glass of clear liquid. I know it's just tonic and lime, but Damon would have you believe differently. His shiny bald head is constantly coated with sweat. I don't ask why, I never ask. I only drift by and nod my head.

"D, what's up."

"Kinda quiet Jake. But it's early. Excellent contribution."

I ignore the last comment and pull Veronika on down the hall. His leer is so heavy with hunger that my own stomach growls. Like she always does, Veronika makes eye contact, her subtle grin an eternal invitation.

"Come on Veronika," I say.

The muffled throb opens up to a dense sound of distant drumbeats and mellow guitar riffs. The room expands into a cavern, a huge room filled with an array of dark lights and metalwork. An open dance floor fills the center, while leather couches run along the walls. Incense fills the air with musk and cedar. A long dark bar is dwarfed by floor to ceiling stained glass windows, a dull glow of red and gold shimmering down to us.

"Drinks?" I ask.

"Yes baby, please. I'm parched. Is anybody here yet?"

"Um...yes, sure. You just have to look close."

We wander to the mahogany bar, leather stools lined up like soldiers, empty souls with endless possibilities. Veronika looks around, soaking it all in. She squints her eyes towards the corners of the room, where cherry tips glow, then fade into nothing. Bits of flesh and fabric squirm into each other, a quiet laugh, and barely audible groan.

"Are they…"

"Maybe. Don't stare Veronika, it's not polite."

"Oh. Sorry. Didn't know there were rules."

"There are rules. And I'll share them with you in just a second. Come sit down."

We glide to the bar, every bit of motion and sound a distraction. Glasses clinking in the darkness, ice cubes sucked and then crunched between teeth, giggles and whispers at the edges of the room.

As we sit down at the massive wooden altar, a figure materializes from the other end of the bar, smoke and a hint of lavender, and jasmine of course. Tightly stretched PVC clings to her body, light reflecting off of her hourglass frame. A dusting of cleavage screams from restriction, her eyes glued to me as she wanders our way.

"Bombay Sapphire martini up with two olives for me, Jasmine, and a Cosmo for my girl here, if you would please."

"Sure, Jake. Whatever you like."

"Thanks. You're the best."

She wanders away to make the drinks, and I watch her move, as Veronika glares my way.

"You know her?" she asks.

"Know her? I know her name. That's all you need to worry about."

"Don't be a dick."

"Look, Veronika. If you're going to be jealous of every glance and caress, then we might as well leave now. It's a little different down here, we talked about that. You cool or not?"

She glances back at the bartender, who shakes the ice and liquor with the aggression of a top, but the willingness of a bottom. Her breasts a constant distraction, but for once, it's okay to stare. She wants me to. She wants Veronika to. She's an exhibitionist. Aren't we all?

"I'm cool, Jake, as a cucumber. She's kind of hot, in a pierced nipple, smack my ass kind of way."

"About that my dear, you are correct."

The drinks arrive, and Jasmine leans over to whisper something in Veronika's ear. I watch her eyes, those green monsters, those fractured diamonds. Her eyebrows go up, and a smile crosses her face. My stomach drops, but it's to be expected. Jasmine continues at her ear, either reciting a dirty limerick, the constitution, or tonguing her lobe into submission. Veronika reaches for her drink, her eyes locked on mine the entire time. Three quick gulps as Jasmine leans over further.

I take a moment to soak up her cleavage, the pale white chasm hypnotic in its spell.

"No," Veronika whispers, and Jasmine pulls away. Her ohawks grin is a beacon in the dark, as she walks back towards me, a flush creeping over her.

"I'll put it on your tab, okay Jake?" she says as she continues on down the bar.

Two leather clad goth boys have appeared at the end. Spiky gelled hair and dark t-shirts with hieroglyphics on them pout over the railing, motorcycle boots and folded arms.

An olive skinned waitress wanders by, barely dressed at all. She's headed to the cage. A burgundy corset holds her small breasts to her, thong panties below are the rest of her outfit. As she drifts past, I nod and smile, and wait for Veronkia's reaction.

"Jacob."

Maybe it's too much. Or maybe I'll lose her. But I knew both of those things already. That's the game, isn't it?

"Jacob?"

"Yes dear?"

"She has a tail."

"Who, Veronika?" I grin.

"The waitress. She has a horses tail shooting out of her ass."

"She does."

"Um...how..."

"Do you really want to know? It's part of her fetish."

"Oh."

"She's very detail oriented. A bit anal you might say."

We stare at each other, and then break out laughing. She's okay, I think. We sip our drinks and I watch her eyes scan the room. She sees the cage in the corner now, and hardly flinches. It's not the restraints so much as it is the whips and branding irons. I wonder how long it will take her to discover the furries in the back of the room. A sharp bark and muffled slobbering brings a smile to my face, but she doesn't hear it.

"Don't you want to know what Jasmine asked me?"

"Oh it's Jasmine now?"

"Yes. She told me her name, Jasmine. Don't you want to know?"

"I know."

"Really? What did she say then?"

"She said you were stunning. She said her name was Jasmine. She said that if you wanted her to lick your pussy like it had never been licked before, to meet her at the back of the bar at 9:30. Then you said no, and gulped down half of your Cosmo."

I'm greeted with silence and a marble gaze. Her jaw clenches and she raises her drink to her barely parted lips, the rest of her crimson lipstick disappearing in a gulp. She squints her eyes, and opens her mouth to speak.

"It's okay, Veronika, she does it to everyone. Well, every hot chick she meets. It's kind of a test to see how new you are to the scene, and how attached you are to me. You're white hot, babe. You know it. I know it. Marcus and Damon know it. The waitress knows it. Even the two bisexual goth boys at the end of the bar know it. It's okay here. Just let it out. That's what we're here for."

"Oh."

I stare at her, caressing her body with my eyes. This is it. The moment.

"I have to use the ladies room."

"It's in the back. Can't miss it."

Veronika gets up and runs her hands down the front of her dress, smoothing out the nonexistent wrinkles. She eases over to me, placing her hot palms on my thighs.

"I'll be right back," she says, leaning over. Her warm lips press against mine, and my breath is gone. Her tongue gently slides into my mouth, and then she pulls away leaving but a trace of her scent, my chest a jackhammer.

"I'll be here."

She walks past me, and I turn to follow her gait. I'm filled with longing, with fear, and then the delicious taste of freedom returns, and I take a deep breath. I look down at my watch.

It says 9:30.

AMAZEMENT

Rubbing my thumb and forefinger over my eyelids, stars shoot across my vision as circles morph into headlights, and the dull thud of his car door fills my head with cotton. Thick brown hair, the color of anticipation on a university campus as the leaves change and fall from the dying frames.

Keys drop onto concrete, and a grunt is followed by a string of mumbling profanities. The ability to hit a fastball, and the ability to strike out fast into the space where contemplation should have sat, regardless of the person in front of me, regardless of age or sex. A penchant for busty women in tight clothes, turning off every warning system, tossing aside every red flag that landed in my grasp. Long fingers that allow me to reach well over an octave on the old upright piano in the beige carpeted living room, next to the red and black brick fireplace. Cookies and carrots, and a glass of milk, year after year after year.

And the ability to hold four bottles of beer in each hand, cold and wet, the only company on many a rain splattered night. Many a hot, muggy summer's yawn. Many a cool, peaceful evening. A string of 842 days. Flecks of gold with the odd green sparkle that always looked forward, never content for a moment, always seeing what could be, what should be, not what is. And for that blindness, the additional gift of fingers that can only let sand sift between them, no matter the fear or grasp. The inability to change the oil, adjust the carburetor, or repair the manifold, a deep seated resentment in the back of that Candy Apple Red '66 Mustang, the naivete and desire of youth fighting against the hatred he instilled in me.

Sitting on the steps in the dark, my ass cold and numb, I wait. Watching him stumble towards me, the brilliance of his ego spins a web of disillusionment around him, a protective coat of armor. Not tonight.

His secretary at the office, accounts payable, accounts receivable. She was my first crush, until she revealed herself to be no more then an ornament and distraction. The bartender on bowling night, my first job unclogging the pins from the machines in the back, every limb flexed and stretched out amidst the trembling framework of metal teeth that yearned to take a bite. Up at the country, the neighbor lady, just stopping by to drop off some venison jerky she'd made from a buck her husband had shot not too long ago.
Glances held a bit too long and wandering eyes that held no remorse.

Nature and nurture. Success and failure. As the heroin coursed through my veins, and my head swam, my body shook and oozed a warmth that was false and fleeting. I could hear his voice, the excuses, the stories. Those tales and yarns that had caused my eyes to widen, my heart to fill with promise, now only shoved the pain beneath my sinuses, into my temples, and down my throat. I was visiting him, here in this lonely garage, his true firstborn, the choice he made so many nights. Revisiting, in many ways.

Or the next five seconds, anyway. Again and again, the noise, the space filled with a cacophony of metal banging, smoke and oil, every night that I had snuck out, and back in again, every hope and dream dashed by his seed. In those moments of brilliant light, he had only one expression for me, amazement. If only I had gotten that look earlier in my life. At any point in time. On the baseball field, at the school play, the graduation ceremony, or book signing, the wedding, or birth or death. Any of it, at any point in time. Just once.

Finally, we would do something together, with perfection, and permanence. My lips wrap around the barrel, the smell of burning flesh, and if only I could feel it. The last muscle tightens, my finger pulls, and there must have been one more flash, one more bang, before I fall on top of him, in a final embrace that was not at all enough to fill the gaps and voids in this young boy's heart.

VICTIMIZED

It's the third night in a row and my bloodlust can't be quenched. There aren't many women here, I'm one of the few. They don't have the stomach for it. I do. This advancement in prison control, this thinning of the herd was inevitable. The people won't stand for anything less. The guilty have an option now at the hands of their victims. There are no laws here, no punishment beyond this place. Fight or die. On some nights, fight and die.

The warehouse is vast and yet we are on top of each other. Some are sweaty, wiping their foreheads with the back of their hands, taking deep breaths. Others have their arms wrapped around emaciated frames, shivering as if cold. In the center of the room is a patch of canvas, a lone dim bulb descending from the rafters, a sepia tone declaring this time history to be recorded. Risers are scattered around the ring, leading up to concrete walls and dusty windows with spiderweb cracks. Mottled red girders extend across the space.

The stench is nauseating, men who haven't bathed in weeks, ripe and rotten. Sweaty socks and rancid feet fill my nostrils. But it is the scent of the man I must beat down in three days, so I inhale deeply, eyes watering. I come to prepare myself, to rid myself of this mark. This idea of victim. This hiding my eyes and looking away. I am here to gain every advantage I can and watch these men become beasts.

I stand at the top of the metal steps. Months I've prepared. Trimming every ounce of fat. Building up muscle where none existed. I fix my gaze on the distance, a place in time where we'll meet again, and he will not know me then, not as he did before.

The bell rings, sharp and crisp. A mumble works its way through the crowd as the two men leave their corners. One is tall and gangly, his bony ribs protruding from his chest.

He moves slowly, one step at a time, watching his opponent, mouth open, hands clenched. Across from him is a cloud of rage, black lines and insects, a sheet of rain occupying the space. It is pent up frustration. It is a blind, numb animal instinct. Must be family. They always look like that, the family of the victims. Dark eyes focused, arms trembling, his aging frame strong and pale. I guess father. He's shaved his head as they often do, a ritual shedding of the past. His lumbering gait is a bit off, balance broken from years of remorse, eons of anguish drowned in buckets of amber.

Voices drift to me. Incest, rape, murder. A sister or daughter? Sex and an accident. A repeated accident. In truth, a plan. Odds are two-to-one in favor of the criminal. He is twenty years younger. Agile and slow, a grin eases across his face. He has faith it will work out. He is wrong.

The men that surround me are all the same. Variations on a theme. The short, dark toad in front of me holds a fistful of bills in one hand and a notepad in the other. Old school.

"Bookman," I say. "Hey, Bookman."

He turns around, glances to my left, to my right, finally to my eyes, as they bore into him.

"What's up, lady. You want some action?"

"100 bucks on the old man. The father."

"You sure, baby?"

I swallow my rage and take a deep breath.

"Just asking..."

I hand him a bill, and he sucks it into his fist, scrawling his mark and some numbers on the pad. His mouth parts in a toothless grin. He blinks and a twitch invades his left eye.

"Here you go."

He tears off the scrap of paper and hands it to me.

I look up in time to see the scarecrow advance, a flurry of fast fists to the old man's head.

Right, right, left, right.

He steps back. Forward.

Jab, jab, cross, uppercut.

Fists pulled back, he hesitates, full of pride and wonder. A grin sweeps across his face, a bounce in his step, this bag of sticks confident, as the balding hunchback straightens up.

The old man pulls his fist from ten years ago, up past his hip, and the crowd goes silent. We all see it. The left-right step, left hand crossing over, then cocking back, right hand moving forward, one smooth motion as if he composed it yesterday. I can't believe I didn't see these paws before. They were hidden on his flank, two sledgehammers at the end of his arms. Right before contact, a second before the stain's nose is smashed into his face, before the blood flows and cartilage snaps, the smile leaves his face. Now he knows. He screwed up.

I feel a tingling sensation between my legs. My mouth opens and I gasp into the foul air, my secret lost in the screams of the room. It will be a long night. I have things to work out. And I won't be alone.

The fist connects, filling the face until I fear it may push through. One shot. That's all it will take. The old man exhales, the grunt of an avenging angel who has fallen so far that the only way is up. Up through the face of the random stranger who took it all away. The thin limbs shoot out as his face crumples in on itself, the nose shifting to one side, a flow of crimson pouring down his face. It covers his chest and seeps into his shorts. Teeth snap, and imbed in the knuckles of the giant fist that has eclipsed the sun. Legs kick out as he falls backwards with an empty thud. A jolt of his legs and he is still, a trickle of urine running out of his shorts, his bare skin pink, before it fades to gray.

Standing over him, the aging hulk wants more. He grabs the flaccid neck and picks it up. Cocking his fist, he holds the scrawny frame, arms trembling, a gust of air flowing out of him. And then another. He drops the man, and steps away, head hung. Turning to the side he retches. Wiping his mouth, he walks away. It is done now, and it was never what he wanted. But he had no choice.

The ape in front of me hands me back three bills and walks down the steps. My winnings will be spent, every cent. I can't have that taint on me. Even in the death of the miserable, the wasted, I cannot celebrate. A smile fills my face as I plan his execution. I will practice tonight on the drunken flesh of the nearest golem.

They all blur together, these memories. Bits and pieces that I repressed for so long. That I chose not to believe, for my sanity. They have something in common, these moments he stole from me, these bits of me he took. They are all wrapped in an uneasy blanket. His hands were hands I trusted.

His caress was one I longed for, out of love, this love of family, the undying depth we had, that filled me up and gave me peace. This ate at me, like a rash on my skin, and I scratched until it bled.

Some nights when I can't sleep, they come to me, these moments. Scattered and grainy, fast cut edits, slicing through the dark sky. In these moments, I am restless and uneasy, and I hear his footsteps in the hall.

"Uncle Jon, is that you?"

"Shhhh baby, I just came to tuck you in."

Crickets out the open window, fireflies flickering in the dark.

"You should be asleep Annabelle. School tomorrow."

"I know. It's too hot out."

"Well take off your nightie sweetheart, I'll help you."

It was always my naked flesh, this innocence that I'd had forever, unable to act any other way. So I never considered what I did, or how he reacted. I didn't think twice about the situations I was in, and how he appeared, a silent ghost on the wind, waiting to help me.

"Aren't you going swimming Anna?"

"I'm coming, just putting my suit on. It keeps getting stuck, the crisscross thingy in the back."

"Here sweetie, I'll help you. You've got it all tangled up. Here, take it off. All the way off. Okay, now turn around and step into it. There you go. You got it now."

Where were my parents? Oh. Right.

He was always eager to help out, to babysit. Go out and have some fun, he'd say. Go see that movie, have some drinks, relax. I'll stay with Annabelle.

"It's okay Uncle Jon, I can do it by myself."

"I know you can, Anna. Just humor me. If anything happened to you, if you slipped in the tub, if you hit your head and drowned to death, well, your parents would never forgive me."

"But..."

"Baby, I've seen it all before. Ain't no big thing. Here, I'll help you wash that long brown hair. It must be a pain in the ass to take care of."

"Sometimes."

"Look, the bubbles are all in there, how fun is that?"

"Uncle Jon, I'm too big for a bubble bath."

"Nonsense, honey. Your mama takes bubble baths. Go ahead and get undressed."

I toss and turn. His hands on me. Were they supporting me, holding me up, helping me? Or were they trapping me, pushing me down, hurting me?

The bad dreams. For so many years. Being chased in the dark, these horrible beasts, trees with long arms, pointy branches, scratching my skin, poking me in the back, poking me in places that were foreign in every way.

I dreamt so hard that some mornings I swear there were cuts on my skin, band-aids I don't remember. Drops of blood in my panties. I didn't understand.

Tonight I lay in my bed, alone. Again. The fight is a distant blur of rust and bone. Years ago it seems. I have blood on my hands again, but it's not my own. No details remain, only his hands on me. Supporting me, holding me up, helping me to undress. His breath rich with bourbon and beer. The walk to my apartment is short, only a step or two, straight to my bed, my clothes falling off me like leaves in an autumn breeze. This dance I am doing now, it is recreating the act, over and over again. Muscle memory. Laughter and hair tossing, a batting of my eyes, and his skinny wrists slip into the handcuffs, a leer creeping over his mouth. Salivating, eager, ready for me, it is this point in the dead of the night, the gap before dawn, that I slip the gag into his mouth, and start cutting. The blade is quiet, a gasp in the night, slicing at arteries, blood spurting as his back arches, screaming into the cloth. I grab hold of whatever I can, cutting it off, slashing deep, gouging the flesh, bathed in sticky syrup, my eyes wide, a stranger to myself.

The crisp white sheets are clean and I'm alone. Again. At peace with the darkness, my eyes closed.

The gravel in the parking lot crunches under my bootheels. The shadow at the door stands with arms crossed, dimly lit by the opening behind him. The muffled sounds of a thousand stomping feet beat behind the thick metal door, a bass drum thudding in sync with my heart.

"Hey Belle, what's up," he says.

He is a mountain of pale, white flesh, bald head littered with scripture, manicured goatee pointing to his chest. I stay with his eyes, watching the pupils jump, as my lips part into a grin.

"Hey Cane. Keeping you busy?"

"You know it. Good crowd tonight. The usual."

"Nothing strange going on?"

"Not yet," he says, eyes drifting down to my skintight jeans, the black half-shirt clinging to my curves.

"The night is young," I say.

"True. You ready for tomorrow?"

"Sure."

"I don't have to worry about you do I? I'll close up the front and come hang if you want..."

"Naw, it's okay..."

"...really I don't mind. Fuck the rules."

I push up against him. It's like trying to hug a redwood. I'm a moth fluttering against an Aztec sun.

"I'm good," I say, the hush barely carrying to him, as he leans over to soak up every syllable.

"Alright. I don't wanna see you get hurt, baby."

We stand still for a moment, him the extended overhang of a dilapidated old building, me the silent furry beast skittering about under the pillars. The door pushes open, letting out a hot rush of sweaty noise. A skinny kid in torn denim and piercings stumbles out, his pockets inside out, knuckles bloody, his gait askew.

"Go. Go on in. Prepare yourself Annabelle."

I ease towards the door frame, leaving his eyes to wander my backside. I can feel his hunger creeping up my spine and consider for a moment the possibilities. No. Too close to home.

Down the long hall, through the boroughs I move, passing one neighborhood and into the next. A huddle of goth whores suck down cigarettes in the corner. A ring of skinheads flex muscles to the right. A pile of retards squat in their own urine. And a trio of flesh peddlers soak up the moonlight, glossy lips like forbidden apples. Closer to the ring the serious boys beat on the mat, leather jackets in black and brown. Bookies and pimps, cokeheads and stoners, MILFS on the prowl and young turks circling, toying with skinjobs.

I can see Michael in the ring. I'm in time. He glances over to me as I pass. I nod and head up the rafters. Eyes on the prize, Mike. Watch your back. Sensing his foe advancing, his head pivots back like a Mastiff tracking its kill. The skeleton halts.

Michael is a legend here. The fighters are mostly family. Furious fathers, beaten down brothers, rage filled husbands, chomping at the bit. All ready to die to avenge somebody. Michael is different. He's none of these things.

When they come up for trial, they're given the choice. Jury or the ring. Most take the ring. There's always the chance that nobody will oppose them. Some of the men, the beasts, they go free without ever stepping on the canvas. If they're smart they go underground and are never seen again. You don't have to stand in the daylight to peddle your wares.

Michael. Right.

I watch him go around and around. He's built like a bulldog, short and squat with a massive neck. He wears these stupid tight black shorts. I'd say he looks gay if I didn't like him so much. Trust him so much. Want him.

So. Much. But he's family. He's not ripped, he's solid. Big arms, the same girth all the way down. Tree trunks for legs. His chest is as deep as my shoulders are wide. Wider. Hairy as a bear. When his black eyes turn to me, I go cold. They always find me, no matter where I stand, no matter what violence is unfolding in the ring. We're kin.

Michael is here every night. He stands in for the weary, the weak. The no-shows. And there are plenty. He used to be a cop, private dick, security. Other. I don't ask anymore. He stands in for those that chicken out, and his beat downs are historic. He has levels. Depending on what you're in for.

It starts at broken bones, and descends from there for the murderers and rapists. The child molesters. Those never leave alive. They never go easy. He offered to take mine for me. I told him no. He understood.

His grunting from the ring brings my vision back into focus. His arms tighten around the thin man's neck. I open my ears to the language of the risers. Drugs, kids, strung along. Thief, violence, death.

Something snaps and the bag of bones stiffens, gargling a request for mercy. Michael twists his arm behind his sharp little back and breaks it. The pale frame collapses in the dust, the mat barely responding to his presence. Both arms are bent behind him at awkward angles, wrong, upsetting. I turn away. It still gets to me. The crowd fills my ears with their rapture. I give Michael a quick glance, my face twisted, lips pursed, nodding nonetheless, giving him my approval. I have to. He needs to receive it, as much as I need to give it.

They clear off the mat as quick as they always do. Very little blood tonight. I scan the crowd quickly, the pause filling my stomach with butterflies.

"She's here," the frogman in front of me says.

"Who?" I ask.

"Your girlfriend. She's here."

"Oh. Cool."

"It's okay baby, I understand."

His lips distend, holding the stub of a cigar, a wisp of smoke drifting up to the brim of his hat.

"It's not like that, asshole."

"Belle. I know. I'm rooting for her too."

He turns around.

More people know me here then I'm comfortable with. Like I've said, not many women. Not here by the ring. Not in the ring. I came to watch her.

To learn, to prepare myself, to hope.

They come out at the same time from different sides of the warehouse. Him in a ratty old bathrobe, twisting his neck from side to side, cracking his knuckles. She drifts to the edge of the mat like a gazelle, slow and graceful, covering the ground in more time than makes sense. She is the light to my dark. Blonde to my brunette. Lipstick lesbian to my bull dyke. She gazes in my direction, holding her right hand over her eyes and I smile with my entire being for the first time in years. And my stomach drops. I fear for her.

They strip off the outerwear, the sweatshirts, the robe. Down to skin and muscle, tight leggings and chestplate hiding her womanly curves, him in tired shorts that are no color but dirt. I told her not to. She isn't ready.

The mumbling in the crowd builds, catcalls and whistles, and the toad turns around, raising one eyebrow in a question.

"No. Thanks."

He turns back around, shrugging his shoulders. Taking the bills and handing out slips. The bell rings.

He goes right for her. I know the stakes. Rape, torture, fracturing her in more ways than I can count. Not that long ago. I see a rabid pit bull advancing on a small white poodle and yet I cannot look away.

His meaty hands go for her neck, eyes bulging, lips in a snarl. She ducks under as he flounders past, shoving her tiny fist into his stomach, knocking out his wind. He slumps over, so she darts back in, peppering his back with a rapid fire attack.

Jab, jab, jab, jab, jab. Pause. Jab, jab, jab, jab, cross.

She backs away, face flush, a smile lighting up her rosy cheeks. His back is littered with red marks, puncture wounds I think. She's wearing something on her hands I can't see. Good girl.

He straightens up, blood trickling down his back. His fists clench and unclench, teeth bared as he advances. She is light on her feet, bouncing around, circling him, always one step ahead and he can't get close. Anger boils to the surface and you can read every word on it. All he wants is to strangle the life out of her, wipe that goddamn smile off her cute little face, bend her over and fuck her, hard.

Again.

He lunges and she moves to the side with ease, dancing on the balls of her feet. She lashes out one quick right catching the back of his head as he stumbles past, opening up a gouge behind his ear.

He wants her so bad his face is purple with blood.

But she won't let him get near her. Laughter erupts from the crowd. His eyes dart to them, breath speeding up. Some kids in the front row, punks with shaved heads, long hairs with eyeliner, ohawks with safety pins shoved through their cheeks. Torn denim and acne scars.

She stops moving and watches him. She watches the punks.

"No," I whisper. "No," I say, louder. Toad turns to me, then back to the ring.

Without looking his right fist tightens. Staring at the handful of kids his right leg bent, as if leaning into the crowd, he launches at her, left leg extending, swinging around too fast for her to move. She squeals, her eyes wide as the fist catches her in the throat, crushing her windpipe. Her fingers splay as arms go wide, eyes rolling up in her head. She stands on her feet for a moment, dazed. He advances and beats her about her head and chest. She doesn't move, against gravity and logic.

Jab, jab, jab.

Uppercut.

And she falls like a cord of wood. He is on her before she even touches the ground. Tearing at her clothes, popping the clasps on her vest, ripping her shirt off, lapping at her pale breasts, tiny pink nipples pointing to the sky. I've gone deaf amidst the screams. I close my eyes so that I don't see more. She knew the risks. She knew the price.

Most of the crowd turns away, disgusted and disappointed. The punks stay, cheering him on. He pulls at her pants and moves to yank them off. A squat figure, dark and solid, slithers onto the stage and pushes a gun in his ear. A quick pop and down he falls, on top of his victim. Not for the first time, but surely the last. The shadow is gone, blending into the crowd. The kids at the ring stand slack jawed and stunned. One bends over and vomits on his feet as the blood soaks into the mat, another layer of life spilled into it. Officials wander on and kick him off of her. They place hands on wrists, on her neck, over her mouth. A stretcher slides under my thin pale girl and they disappear her into the night. I look for Michael in the crowd, his usual spot, the exact opposite of mine, across the way, low, by the ring. He is gone.

Back then we moved around a lot. But he always seemed to find us. Find me. Standing alone at a bus stop in the rain, smoking a cigarette outside a coffee shop, wandering around outside school.

I wondered sometimes if he was real.

A gas station outside Kansas City waving the heat off me while the nicotine and tobacco bits coated my throat. Parched and sweaty, a long black car would pull up and down the window would go.

"Get in, Belle," he'd say.

And I would. I don't know why. I was bored. He'd buy me beer. He'd let me drive whatever hot rod he had, silver steel and leather, candy-apple red and the smell of oil. It got me hot. He knew it.

Walking out of a bar in Fargo, black knit cap pulled tight, oxblood leather boots stomping into the snow drifts, out of money and patience. Up would pull a battered old gunmetal blue pick-up truck, and in I'd jump. A pint of cheap bourbon, not even a label on it, just scratched glass and brown liquid. The streetlights bouncing off the copper madness, pulling it down my throat as if gasping for air. He'd hand me a gun and we'd pull to the side of the road. He'd reach across me, one hand landing on my thigh, the other rolling down the window.

I'd stick it out the gap and holding it with two shaky hands, fire, blasting a hole in the stop sign, and off we'd drive, peeling around the corner, rubber burning, back-end swaying, cackling in the night like a couple of old hens.

And every morning I'd wake up in my own bed, in nothing but my white cotton panties and an old black Ramones t-shirt. It scared me the first time it happened. Every alarm in my head went off, every inch of my stomach lined with knots and the threat of purging. And yet I was numb to do anything. Except cut myself.

On the nights that he wouldn't show, and there were many, on the cold, dark winter nights I'd run the razor blade over my translucent flesh and mark the occasion, slicing open the thin layer of skin until it beaded with blood, and ran down the side of my arm. Then I'd go out. And I'd find a wayward soul worse off than mine and eat it. I'd do to some poor sap what had been done to me, over and over again. I'd bury one waif in an empty grave. I'd lay another over the train tracks. I'd fling a third over my shoulder and toss the broken colt into a dumpster, the stench of rotten milk and kitty litter floating up to me. And I'd cry. I'd cry until the mascara ran down my face and neck into my cleavage, staining my breasts with the empty depth of my frantic scrambling, my howling at the moon and lost nights. I couldn't stop. His face was on every skull that I broke.

Sinuous. That's the word I am looking for. I stand in front of the floor length mirror, and stare at my naked body. Twenty pounds of muscle replace twenty pounds of fat. I am preparing to go to war and need only apply the paint.

I hold the razor blade up to the dim light, shades drawn, a slice of sunshine piercing through the gaps. I have emptied out this space I inhabited. If I ever really existed here. There is nothing of mine left, for I I may not return. I may have to run. There is only the bed, the stained mattress a study of my history, a Petri dish boxspring stuck to the floor. The dresser, beaten and chipped, the way I found it.

Names my father used to call me: princess, bunny, doodlebug, sunshine, honey, baby, sweetheart, angel.

I slide the blade down my left bicep and forearm, all the way to the wrist. Just enough to break the skin. Then I do the other arm. Down my ribcage, the bones protruding, just a fraction deeper, a bumpy ride to my navel. Bending over it glides down my left thigh and then my right. I stand up straight and place the sticky razor on the dresser. I run my hands over the seeping cuts on my arms, and spread the paint around. I'm an Indian now, redskin.
I dip my right index finger in the expanding droplet at my knee, and paint a line under my left eye. Then my right.

Names my mother used to call me: whore, tramp, slut, loser, waste, darling, pervert, sick.

Leaning against the black GTO, I run my hand over the edge of the hood, back and forth. 1968. Blue jeans and that damn Ramones shirt screaming I want to be sedated. I wasn't even a gleam back in '68, but this girl has the curves, the muscle, and I'd been drawn to her for a long time. She used to belong to my father. Kind of like me. I lift the clear glass bottle to my lips and sip at the liquid gold. Just a little to steel my nerves. A pint to nip at. I won't vomit again.

A crunch of gravel behind me, but I don't turn. It's early still, the sun hasn't even set over the horizon yet, and I stare at the orange dust over the warehouse, as it slowly darkens, the light slipping away. I don't turn because I know who it is. It can only be one person this early.

"You ready, honey?" he asks.

"No."

"Little courage, huh?"

"Just a little, Bookman."

"Make sure it stays that way. You gotta be sharp tonight."

"I know."

I turn to him, and he is ancient. Or maybe I've become fourteen again.

Wrinkled skin and liver spots and I suddenly feel sorry for him, eeking out a living here, watching the blood spill, skimming off the top.

"So what am I up to?"

"Huh?"

"The odds Book. What am I up to?"

"Well, you know...after last night..."

I smile.

"What is it? Twenty? Thirty-to-One?"

"I haven't taken a dime yet, Belle, but it'll be fifty-to-one to open."

I exhale. They have no faith.

"Here. Take it."

I hand him a roll of money. I'm not even sure how much it is.

"I'll either be rich or I'll be dead, Book. Just take it."

"Okay."

He stares at me, eyes bulging.

"Good luck."

The roar of the crowd is deafening, my ears washed over by the weight of the ocean. He stands across from me, eyes glazed over, a sparkle buried there, as his head fills with the past.

I am a deception, an illusion, I am not what I seem. The black spandex shorts and tight sleeveless t-shirt are a very thin mesh, a chainmail of sorts. They cannot be penetrated with a knife. It took me awhile to find the other device, but it still exists. Chastity belt. It is surprisingly comfortable and simple to wear. Thin, pliable rubber, lined with metal braces. There is a slot to urinate, but not to penetrate. He will not violate me if I lose. Not again.

I place the rubber mouthpiece in, and crack my neck from side to side. His heavy stare has been on me since I stepped in the ring. Practically salivating, this blood of mine. A sheen of sweat coats my body, as I shake out my legs, as if ready to sprint. I shake out my arms, and crack my knuckles, wrists taped tight, my smoking gun buried over the scarred flesh, waiting for the final act to reveal itself.

He is not impressive. He is less than I remembered, and a part of me feels sorry for him. A small part. The part of me that liked his hand on my thigh, the part of me that turned a blind eye to his indiscretions. In my mind's eye I see a faucet, with two silver handles on either side. There is hot scalding water streaming out of the opening. I reach over and turn it off.

I finally allow myself to look out into the crowd, to see the faces of my enemies, my neighbors, my chorus. My addiction. They want me to lose, to be torn asunder and punished for my beauty, for simply being a woman. They want to see him get beaten down by the lesser sex. This fickle school of remoras is waiting for the chum to hit the waves, for us to tear each other apart. They will get their wish.

I know Michael is here, I feel his eyes as well. His is a mountain range, a presence on the periphery, and if I look at him I will turn to stone. I am weak, I am strong. I am nothing, I am everything. I take the chance and find his concern, and embrace it. His eyes are ice cubes, blocks of cold disdain. In reality they are holding down his worries and doubts. Like me, he keeps it buried, for fear of letting that weakness destroy him. One simple nod is all he gives me, and it is all that I need.

The bell.

It has started, and I am not ready. I cannot move. My arms hang at my sides as he slowly approaches me, a hyena laughing, his head bobbing up and down, as he eases up to the kill that lies rotting in the African sun. I have forgotten my plan. I have forgotten the face of my father. Uncle Jon advances anyway.

I watch him as he lumbers forward, more fragile now then I remember him, but still very capable of beating me to a pulp. I cannot lift my arms, they are encased in cement. Panic washes over me, and there is nothing I can do. I do not hear the crowd, I hear the screen door slide open, I hear crickets in the back yard chirping, I hear a dog up the street bark and cigarette smoke fills my nose. The crisp snap of a beer can opening and a chuckle in the dark.

He raises his fist and punches me in the face.

It is dark again. As if underwater, sound fades in and out, deep murmurings like a tape being played backwards, and the sharp tingling of needles on my skin, panic, and I open my eyes. His face is all I can see, his mouth open wide, crooked yellow teeth and dry cracking lips. I reach up my hands and shove my thumbnails into his eyes.

And the world rushes back in. I choke on my own blood as he falls off of me, so I turn my head to the side and spit. My mouthguard is gone. My nose may be broken.

A hive of bees fills my face, buzzing while the dull stinging spreads to my cheeks. Placing my hands beneath me I am up as fast as I went under. The room swims, and I take a quick glance around, to remind me of where I am, and why I'm here. Jon writhes on the canvas, holding his face in his hands. Over to Michael, again a quick nod.

One cautious foot in front of the other, I ease over to him. On his hands and knees, still holding his face, a dull moan escapes his lips. I kick him as hard as I can in the chest. He flips over like a turtle on the side of the road.

"Get up," I say.

His eyes blink open, they are still intact. He can still see.

"Get up, you stupid man."

He scrambles back like a crab on all fours, grabs a hold of the ropes and pulls himself up. He blinks again, the flesh around his eyes gouged, bleeding, but his eyes are still on me.

"Goddamn, Annabelle. And after all I did for you, sugar."

I raise my fists and come after him. I pummel his head, but he has raised his arms, and the blows glance off his bony forearms. I pause, he lowers. I sock him in the left eye. Moving too slow, as I go in again, a gray blur fills my vision and he punches me again. I reel backwards, stumbling, but regain my balance.

"Come on, Jon," I say. "This is it."

He moves forward, a bounce in his step.

The initial shock has worn off, but he still thinks this is a joke. Still thinks that deep down he will prevail, no matter what. I'm just a little girl, after all.

When he gets close enough I move to Plan B. A roundhouse kick to the head catches him off guard, sending teeth flying, littering the grimy canvas like a box of spilled Chiclets. Holding his hand to his face, his mouth a bloody gash, I keep coming. A step, a hop and a kick to his chest, the ribs cracking, giving way as his breath flies out of him, staggering back. One more step and a kick to the face, my heel connecting with his nose, head snapping back, blood spraying the air. Drops land on me, my face, spatter my arms and chest as he bounces off the ropes and collapses on the floor.

Standing over him, he lies on his side, a pool of blood forming by his head. The crowd is screaming, they want me to finish him off. But I'm not ready yet. It's not enough.

"Get up," I say. "Get up, you sick fuck."

Slowly he stands up, pushing himself to his knees, grabbing hold of the ropes again, up tall and proud now, his face mangled, eyes swelling shut.

"Let's go you bitch," he says.

I back up.

"Sweetest piece of ass I ever had," he gasps.

I deflate like a balloon. It has been said, out loud. It has a name, it has been called out.

"You used to writhe under me like a worm in the sun," he says, a crooked grin spreading over his face.

I back up further to the center of the ring.

"You'd grab a hold of my ass and tell me faster...harder...give it to me baby!"

My arms fall to my sides, my stomach a knot of twisted muscles and sharp pains.

"And you kept coming back for more."

I stop and stare at him and he raises his fists. My head snaps back and forth, and all I see are his knuckles retreating, and a moment later, the pain reveals itself. A pause and he takes a breath and he does it again.

Left, right, left.

I can't feel my face. My vision is white snow, television noise at three in the morning. My left hand reaches over as he takes another breath. I peel off the tape without even looking at it. I've done it a hundred times. In my tiny little apartment, in front of the mirror. I've done it with my eyes closed. Blind, much as I am right now. I peel off the layer of tape and expose the smoking gun, in this the third, but not final, act. I snap open the straight edge razor in my right hand, down by my thigh, and he doesn't even notice.
He's moving in for the kill. And so am I. He thinks I am dazed, lost, a wounded deer caught in the headlights.

When he takes that final step, and pulls back his right arm, I have my gap, my moment. And I take it. Instead of a rag doll waiting for him to pick me up and set me in his bed, I lunge forward, swinging my right arm with every saved up scrap of rage. The blade slices the air as he steps into it, cutting across his throat, my wrist bending, hurting as it connects, cutting through. The gash opens his flesh up, passing through cartilage, opening his windpipe, his head lolling back. His fist glances off the side of my head as the weight of the punch pushes him forward, bathing me in his fluids for the last time. His heart still pumping, the artery shoots the dark liquid into the air, over my head, as he twists away, holding his hands to his neck. Blood surges over his splayed fingers, eyes wide, choking, spitting blood.

Our eyes.

None of it plays back, only the hissing of air as my mind collapses. A tone rings in my ears as I blink my eyes.

He wants no forgiveness, for in his mind, he did nothing wrong. To him, I was an accomplice, a keeper of his dirty little secrets, aiding and abetting.

His enabler.

He falls to his knees and I say nothing to him. Pointless.

He falls on his face, blood racing across the canvas, creeping into the fabric, and my arms are made of lead.

There must be screaming, there must be something, but I am deaf. I am stone. Down my face flow my tears and I stare at my uncle, my lover, my teacher.

I am grateful for none of it. I am rotten and diseased.

It was many years later when I returned to the ring. They led me in the back door this time, with an escort. Not for Jon, for the others. I was famous now. They didn't want any trouble. I was the only woman to ever win here. I'm a little older now. Still in fighting shape. I've been riding the wind, moving around, lost, unable to settle down. Like oil and water, the real world and I don't mix. Up the back stairs, dark concrete, cold and damp, like sweat socks traipsing through a rain filled gutter.

It's the match of the night, the main event. The building is packed, overflowing into the parking lot, cars on the gravel, spilling into the grass and dirt. Stomping boots, pounding fists, bursting at the seams for my return. When I enter the light, my mouth parts and a smile crosses my lips.

My entourage brings me through the ropes, holding my shoulders, my head so I don't fall. And hurt myself.

I laugh. A quiet laugh.

They undo the handcuffs and out of habit I rub my wrists. They take off my robe, and I am in simple prison garb, the gray shorts and tight tank-top, pale flesh breathing fresh air. Across the ring our eyes connect. Standing inside the ropes, Michael gives me one nod.

TWENTY-DOLLAR BILL

Waukegan, IL

The Trojan horse twenty dollar bill sits in a pile on the night stand. Peeling wallpaper, and thick grey curtains block out the cars rambling by on the interstate. A cigarette smolders in the ashtray as she pulls on her panties. Black lace. Predictable, but effective. I watch her as she dresses, mesmerized by her tight body. Every bend and stretch, the first female flesh I've seen or touched in eleven years. Besides my wife. She is everything that my wife is not. Blonde hair down to her supple ass, green piercing eyes that sparkle when she laughs, and firm breasts that hold my every glance. It's been easier than I thought it would be. Hit the ATM, a stack of bruised green bills, and that one crisp new $20, sitting on top. Watching me, laughing. The paper trail mocks me, screams out adulterer, liar. I don't care. Her name is Kelly, and I think I've found a new hobby. She's gentle and kind and looks me in the eye. Glancing back at me, she smiles, her lips barely parted, head bowed in a shy flush. She's new. I know that much. And I'm already playing back in my mind every motion and touch, every gasp and moan. It'll have to last me. At least until next month. I never notice the blinking red light in the upper right corner of the room. Soon we'll be on the internet. And it will all fall apart.

Waukegan, IL to Libertyville, IL

This john, he's my first, and I have emerged renewed, invigorated, and to a lesser degree, satisfied. Wrapping my long black wool coat around me, my skin hums, and the deep glow from my center is part orgasm, part love, and part hope that I can leave now, be independent. Leave my worthless man. I've finally found my calling. The wasteland around me is nothing but skeletal trees and snow banks with dirty feet, icy and black. Boarded up storefronts and gas stations, overflowing dumpsters and cold, crisp air.

RICHARD THOMAS

The salt splattered Camry waits for me, like nobody does. She's my safe haven in any storm, and as my long black boots clomp across the parking lot, heel-toe, heel-toe, a heat rises up the back of my neck.

He'd been my first, sure, but there's a long line of men waiting in my in-box. They find me attractive, even if he doesn't. They want to spend time with me, even if he doesn't. They'll help me pay my bills, get the heat turned back on, get the water turned back on, get the fucking phone and internet turned back on. They've got me turned back on. Pulling out a handful of keys, I open the beige door. Exhaust from a semi passing by coats me in soot, grounding me in the reality of the moment, and ripping me out of the film in my head. Off to the Currency Exchange. Bills to pay. Or not. Maybe it's time to leave. Fuck him. He can deal with it all. Whenever he comes home. Whenever he wakes up. It'll be a quick stop. Two suitcases, and my laptop. A pot or two. That's all I need. The rest I have. In my head. And in my skirt. That hot, moist moment of pleasure that men will kill to get at. Pay to get at. I have the power now, and nobody is going to take it away again. Pulling into the Wendy's I order a #1 with cheese, large diet coke. Hungry, in so many ways. Here's a $20.

Libertyville, IL to Chicago, IL

If you're real smart, and fast, you can take the order at the drive through window, not enter it into the register, and verbally relay that to the fry cook. You can steal that twenty dollar bill and issue the change directly from your previous transactions, straight out of your pocket. No one is the wiser. Crisp, folded in half, slipped into my jeans. She was hot though, in a MILF kind of way. Bit of pale cleavage leaking out of that bundled up coat, a ray of sunshine in that suburban soccer-mom car, winter beating at the window, her smile a hint at something more. I almost say something. Totally out of character. Like, what are you doing later? Like, what's your sign, hot mama? Please. I get enough ridicule in school, I don't need it from some hottie on her way home from Pilates class. Even if that bit of thigh slicing out from under her long black coat will probably drive me to self-abuse later. Probably. Most definitely. What else do I have going on? I pull the bill back out, after she's driven off, after her order has been filled, a gap in the lunch rush as things ease up. Even in the middle of the grease, the onions, the charred beef, garlic, and oil, it has a hint of her on it. A hint of something musky and sweet. It's almost more than I can handle. I'll sniff it while I sit on the train, headed back to the city to meet up with my brother. Working at Wendy's when you're in High School is one thing. Working at Wendy's in college is another.

Working at Wendy's when you're 30 is a disgrace. I won't give this to the conductor. Or the homeless guy with no legs who sits in his wheelchair on the Washington bridge crossing over the Chicago River. I have singles for him, and a nod of the head, a momentary locking of our eyes. His warning to me. My understanding to him. Don't go there. Don't come here. I won't. Good. I'll hand this to my older brother. His long brown hair shaggy with waves, greasy and thick. The bar code tattoo on his left wrist flashes for a moment as he takes it, quickly, never looking me in the eye. It covers up the scars there, at his wrist. The black ink hides the scar tissue, the cuts horizontal in hesitation, vertical when it was serious. It's all I can do. He's pale, and shivers, no matter how many thrift store flannel shirts I bring him. No matter how many black sweatshirts. He always looks cold. And it's contagious. I head back to the train. Back home to the suburbs, to mom and dad, the clinical dinner table, lack of commentary, lack of discussion. He doesn't come up. I don't bring him up. Our eyes meet over passed butter and ladled gravy. My brother. I hope he's eating.

Chicago, IL

So many choices. El Chino Burrito. A fifth of Old Grand Dad. The electricity bill. Socks. A hand job. I stand at the intersection of lost and found, blurs of yellow screaming by on their way to airports or high rise eruptions. It's too cold to smell a thing, my nose hairs crisping in the frigid air. She said she'll do me this favor. If I help her move. If I help her get away from him. I know the story. I've seen the bruises. Hands shoved deep in my coat pockets, the crumpled up bill clenched with the others. I gave blood. I gave sperm. I gave gold fillings to the man on the corner with the little shop that asks no questions. The crusty blood dried at the corner of my chapped lips. His eyes stare, looking down, then up then gaze back down again. His knuckles are hairy, short stubby fingers, ringed with gold, and sparkling stones, his work. No more, he says. Stop it, he warns. I nod and leave. In my pockets, my long slender fingers that used to play, at so many things. Keyboards. Guitar strings. Typewriters. Sweaty necks, rubbing lower, closing my eyes, getting paid. She said if I helped her to escape him that she'd cut me a deal. No freebie, I was not a symphony. A sympathy. A discount for a preferred customer, a friend maybe. A warm body. I stand there in the cold, every slice of the sky blue or gray, every bit of structure metal or glass. But I stand. She pulls up in the long beige sedan, right on time. Or is it hours too late? There isn't much to get, she says. Some boxes, some clothes maybe. But we have to hurry.

No more waiting for the fists to land, the rotten stench of his breath in her mouth. No more, she says. But we have to hurry. I climb into this foreign ship, this tan piece of suburbia, familiar is so many ways to a life I once knew. It's warm. She smells of sandalwood and sweet spices, brown sugar and patchouli. Hiding in her long dark coat, her blanket of wool and sanity, her shelter from anything that could actually touch her. I reach out my hands to her as she cups hers under mine. Down comes the rain, the crumpled up ten dollar bills, the fives, and the one folded, crisp twenty. Is it enough? It is.

INTERVIEW

1 SAMSON REINFORCED 60" X 36" FOLDING TABLE: $236.14

The doorbell rings throughout the quiet house as she stands outside underneath the one dim bulb. Waiting on the front porch she takes in the view of the nice, suburban street lined with oak trees and 4-door sedans. Her own battered grey Corolla sits in the driveway ticking. He opens the door.

"Hi how are you, so glad you could make it."

"Hi Mr. Thompson."

"Come on in Sariah. Is that how you say it? Suh-rye-uh?"

"Exactly. Like Sarah, but with an I."

He holds open the screen door for her as she squeezes past him into the foyer. Her jeans are tight. Her pink short-sleeve shirt reads JUICY. Her long blonde hair is pulled back in a ponytail, and she looks kissed by the sun. Green eye shadow completes her face.

1 BOX OF HEFTY CINCHSAK TRASH BAGS, LARGE 30 GALLON, 32 CT: $7.99

"Well, how long has it been? You mean you keep track?" she asked.

"I didn't use to. Then I started to get angry about it, and I wanted to see exactly what was going on. So I'd have some ammunition for this very conversation. This year, we've had sex three times. I can give you the exact moment of each: Valentine's Day, the weekend in Lake Geneva, and whatever went right six weeks ago when we went out for Mexican."

"Oh that's absurd. That can't be right."

"Oh it is. Do you know how many times we did it last year?"

1 PAIR OF PLAYTEX HANDSAVER LATEX GLOVES, LARGE: $2.19

"Here, follow me into the living room. Sorry the place is such a mess, I was just cleaning up after the twins. They're a handful at times, but I love them!"

"Oh, it looks fine. Here, I'll help you with those Matchbox cars." When she bent over to pick up the 1966 Silver Corvette and the 1967 Red Mustang, her jeans stretch down, revealing a black thong.

"Thanks. Here, you can just put them in the case. Sit down. And sorry it's just me, my wife is out of town on business, she travels a lot, and the kids are already asleep."

"No problem."

"Do you want a soda or something? We have Diet Dr. Pepper, Sprite, and Coke. And bottled water, Evian."

"Water would be fine, thanks Mr. Thompson."

"Please, call me Jeff. You're making me feel ancient. I'm only 35."

1 BOX OF TROJAN CONDOMS, MAGNUM, LARGE SIZE, LUBRICATED, 12 CT: $7.19

"No, but I'm sure you do."

"8 times."

"That's a lie..."

"No, it isn't. We were doing good for awhile there, once a month up until June. Then it petered out, if you'll pardon the expression. You know, the holidays, travel for work, all that stuff. I mean, I'm 35 not 65."

"Well, I can't help it when I'm out of town. What am I supposed to do, call up and give you phone sex? Play with myself in some strange dirty hotel room while you whip it out here in the kitchen?"

"That's one idea."

"Oh you're sick. I'm not going to do that."

"You don't do a lot of things. Any more."

1 2 OZ. VIAL OF GAMMA HYDROXYBUTYRIC ACID (GHB) WITH SYRINGE: $250.00

"Here's your soda, Sariah. So how long have you been babysitting?"

"Well, you know I'm a junior at Jefferson High School, across the street."

"Right. I sent your choir director, Mrs. Blanche, an e-mail, and she posted that notice on the job board. That's how I found you."

"And, well...I've been watching my younger brother and sister for as long as I can remember. All by myself for a couple of years now."

"So you think you can handle the twins? It takes a lot of energy to keep up with them. They wear me out sometimes."

"No problem. I'm in gymnastics, so I stay in shape. I like to jog, and like I said, I'm always chasing my brother and sister around, so it's probably about the same."

"So what do you do for discipline, how do you deal with the kids when they're acting out?"

"Well, whatever you think is best...um, Jeff," smiling, pushing a strand of hair behind her ear. "I usually do time outs, and I definitely never hit them, or spank them. I don't even like having to grab their arm or anything, um...unless they're gonna run out into the street or something."

"OK. That sounds good. Is it ok with your mom and dad to babysit on a school night or only on the weekends? And do you have a curfew or anything?"

"Um...well, it's just my mom. They divorced a couple of years ago. My dad lives up in Minnesota, and we see him on the weekends now and then. But mostly it's my mom. She's ok with it if I let her know where I am. I think maybe 11:00 on school nights, but I can probably say later, say 12:00 or 1:00 on the weekends."

1 MAKITA 18 VOLT CORDLESS RECIPROCATING SAW: $326.99

"You used to offer me a lot of favors. Promises. If I did something for you, you'd give me a little extra special attention. Do you know how many IOU's I have upstairs in my drawer?"

She laughs. "No Jeff, no idea. I'm guessing a lot."

"I don't even know myself. But that drawer is full of them. What good are they? Like you'd honor them. If I brought you one right now, would you help me out? Take care of me?"

"Jeff...I'm not in the mood right now. What...we're fighting, so I'm just supposed to turn off my emotions and jump on you? I can't do that."

"Funny. You have no problem turning on the TV and laughing at some stupid show after a long day. No problem loading up a plate with Taco Bell or Arby's, followed by strawberry ice cream."

"Hey...that's not the same thing. It doesn't take any work to do that.
And you're not exactly in perfect shape yourself, are you."

"No. I weigh 215 pounds. At 6'2" that's maybe 15 pounds overweight. What do you weigh?"

"That's none of your business," her face at once stoic.

"I think it IS my business. You weigh 194, Susan."

"What...you don't know what you're...where do you get that number, that's absurd."

"You know the high-tech scale we have, that you HAD to have? Not only gives you your weight, but your body mass index and all that? Well, when you step on the scale, it flashes the last weight for a second. I thought I'd lost a lot of weight. I was all excited. Until I realized it was you."

1 AMES TRUE TEMPER CLASSIC ROUND POINT SHOVEL: $14.99

"Sounds great. Do you like to cook? Nothing fancy, you know Mac and Cheese, Hot Dogs, pasta, stuff like that. Can you handle a knife?"

"Oh sure, I love to cook. I do it all the time for my brother and sister. Mom has to work at nights sometimes, so I help out. I don't mind. Grilled cheese, Chicken Noodle Soup, and I make a mean Rice-A-Roni," she laughed, her blue eyes sparkling.

Jeff smiled, watching her body language for anything gone astray. "Awesome. Love it. Can you give the kids a bath? I'll show you how to do it, it's no big deal, but obviously you have to be careful, they could fall and hit their head, or drown, so you have to stay with them, be very attentive."

"No problem. With my brother and..."

"...sister you do it all the time, right, I forgot."

"That's ok."

"Well, you sound great, Sariah. Anybody that sings in the choir is ok with me. What are you, soprano or alto?"

"Alto. I just can't hit those high notes, I guess."

"I was a tenor myself, sang all the way through college."

"Wow, that's great."

"Are you going to audition for any of the musicals this fall?"

"I don't know, maybe."

"You should, it's lot of fun."

1 PAIR ATLAS NITRILE GARDEN & WORK GLOVES, CORNFLOWER BLUE, LARGE: $6.49

She stared at him, boring two eyes into his forehead. Her eyes glistened.

"Well I don't have time to exercise either I guess. I'm always tired, my job just wears me out. Besides, you have your movies, and the internet. Why don't you just take care of it yourself?"

"I do. And frankly I'm sick of it. And it's not just the sex, believe it or not. It's the intimacy. I don't feel like we ever connect. We're practically brother and sister. We get up, get the kids fed and dressed, then its off to pre-school, and me to work. I work all day, pick up the kids, then home to dinner. Play with the kids, give them a bath, them some dumb TV and then bed. You're either working out of the house, in the city, or out of town. We never have time for each other. And that's not good. I can see this leading to a divorce when the kids are older. Or an affair. And that's not what I want, any of it."

1 10 OZ TUBE OF PURPLE ASTROGLIDE LUBRICANT: $19.99

"Well, as far as I'm concerned, you've got the job. I can't show you the entire house, since the kids are sleeping, but I can give you a little tour. We want you to be comfortable here, we have TiVO, so you can watch whatever you want: MTV, VH1, HBO. You can eat whatever we have. There's ice cream, frozen pizzas, fruit, bagels. If you want something special, let me know and I'll pick it up the next time I'm at the grocery store."

"Sounds great."

"Here, let me show you the back yard." Jeff opened the sliding glass door and screen revealing a nice size back yard with a large wooden swing set, a stone patio, and a garden next to the house. It was partially dug up at the moment. "Sorry about the mess here, we're planting some bushes and I ran out of time. That big hole there is going to house three lavender bushes, if I can get it done tomorrow."

"Nice yard. Much bigger then ours. I love to garden, I help my mom plant tulips every fall"

"That's sweet of you. We do the same out front."

"Oh, here, come on. Let me show you the basement. We just got it finished. The kids love it down there. That way we can leave all of their toys out and not trip over them. It's great." Jeff headed back into the house. He opened the door to the basement. "Go on down, I'm right behind you."

"OK. Oh this is nice. When did you get it all done?" she said, as he closed the door behind them.

The baby monitor buzzed on the counter, as one of the twins coughed and turned over.

RICHARD THOMAS

1 MAKITA 18 VOLT CORDLESS M-FORCE 1/2" DRIVER-DRILL: $189.99 (REDUCED)

"Well why don't you just get a mistress then. You know the medication I take effects my libido, when I'm not exhausted from work. Maybe I'd should get off the Lexipro. Would you like me better like that?"

"Not really. You were impossible."

"I don't know what to say Jeff. I love you, but I just don't know what to do."

"Me either."

"Would a hobby help? At least you wouldn't be bored. I'll talk to my doctor and see if he can prescribe something else. Maybe it isn't just me."

"OK. "

1 BAG OF INDUSTRIAL GRADE LYE, 25 POUNDS: $24.99

The phone rings five times and then goes to voicemail.

"Hi Mr. Thompson, this is Heather. I got your number from Mrs. Blanche, she said you were looking for a babysitter? I live near by, go to Jefferson of course, and I'm in the choir too, duh. I'd love to come by this week. I have varsity cheerleading practice Tuesday and Thursday, but other then that I'm free. Give me at call at 847-123-4857 and ask for Heather. Thanks, and have a great night."

PAYING UP

The yearbook sits in the trunk of my 1967 Camaro, moonlight reflecting in the royal blue. Rusted out wheel wells and torn black leather seats mar an otherwise classic beauty. The dented silver book sits next to a half empty case of warm Coors, six road flares, and a red rag speckled with sawdust, stained with motor oil. The collection of memories spits in my face every time I open the trunk, which is why I put it there.

It isn't mine.

Running my hand along the warm hood, I head toward the entrance of The Dollhouse. I finally tracked her down, and am not sure what it'll become. Butterflies with razor blade wings flit around in my stomach slicing at my guts. I finish off the pint of Jim Beam and toss it into the weeds that line the gravel parking lot. I hitch up my blue jeans and stomp closer to my baby. Worn out combat boots, gray at the edges, soles cracked and frayed, propel me forward as I shake the cotton out of my head, praying for strength.

Doesn't work.

"Hey pops," the doorman says, nodding his bald dome. "Nice wheels."

I slip him the $10 and walk on by. He doesn't know me, but he thinks he does. At least he doesn't call me grandpa. I prefer silver fox when asked, but nobody does. The ladies like it, because they think I have money. I don't. Why else would an aging stud like myself be here. I don't give off the molester vibe, not any more. Tan skin, callused hands, and a beaten up old oxford, they don't say much.

They say enough.

It's every strip club I've ever been in. Mirrors, always a sale on mirrors. College punks up close, dropping the singles on the stage like they mean something, eager to get a face full of tits. Not that I can disagree, really.

The bass pumps, my heart with it, and a bar lines the wall to my right. Shiny bottles full of distraction, a whiff of baby powder as a young filly saunters by, white eyes and curious smile. Her body is lost on me. I am a puppy to her, safely on a leash, yet dead inside.

"Bud," I say at the bar.

I toss another ten spot, and take the cold drink. It goes down fast, and eases my pulse. She's on the center stage when I walk in.

There is no mistaking her. Long brown hair, doe eyes, her mother's shoulders, wide and thick, worn down to nothing, in a glittery black thong, her ass shaking back and forth. I look away fast, a gut full of shrapnel.

"Bud," I say, tossing out more green.

Over to the stage, and I can't hear anything. Deafening silence. She won't know me. I'm counting on that.

"Darla," the disc jockey says, "give it up for Darla, one more song, come on guys, show her you care."

I sit down, the wad of bills in my hand, damp already. She won't take it any other way, I know that. I've tried. She hates me with all of her black little heart, and I deserve it. It's my entire paycheck for the week. $220. It doesn't look like much. I finish the beer and stand back up. Can't do it. I leave the money on the stage, and head for the door, and I can feel her eyes on the back of my head, boring in, questioning, a crooked grin on her face. I don't get to see her smile. I don't get to talk to her. Darla is not her name. Not her birth name, anyway.

I stand at the back of the Camaro, tears streaming down my face, and I turn to vomit, spraying the rocks and my shoes, not for the first time. Straightening up, I take out the yearbook. High school, back when she was still innocent, and I was just becoming a stranger. I stare at her doe eyes and crooked grin. And apologize to my daughter one more time.

TEN STEPS

[1.]

"I never wanted him in the first place," he says, his voice lowering to a hush. "Was all your idea, Becka."

"That's not true and you know it," she says.

"Move in with me, get me a ring, put a baby in me. You never said those things?"

"I don't know."

"Of course you did."

"Well, we've got him now," she says.

Their eyes turn to the crib, the baby's sweaty hands gripping the wooden slats, eyes wide. The silence hangs heavy around them.

"I can't stand looking at his needy little face," he says, walking towards the fridge.

"He's your son, how can you say that?"

"Ask my dad. He can explain it to you."

[2.]

"No, I can't go out, you know that," she says.

The phone in her hand is getting slippery, her eyes darting back and forth from the empty glass of wine to the tiny chest that raises and lowers under a dingy blue blanket and footie pajamas.

"No, I can't do that."

She rubs the back of her neck.

"I've been there more times than you have. I know everyone in there. You know my situation."

She rubs her lower back.

"Three months."

A tiny cough slips from the crib.

"He was an ass. And no, never was any good at that. Had to take care of that myself, too."

She cackles into the phone.

"Just one?"

Outside the wind gusts, rattling the apartment windows.

"Five minutes? It'll never be five minutes."

The little man rolls over.

"Sound asleep. Bobby's not going anywhere."

His eyes open a crack.

"Five minutes, that's it. Just one glass and then I'm coming right back. Doesn't make me a monster does it?"

He closes his eyes. When the door clicks shut his lower lip starts to tremble.

[3.]

"Just watch the tv, honey, I'll only be a minute."

She pulls the man toward the bedroom. He tips his baseball hat at Bobby, a crooked grin under his bushy mustache. The door shuts, a lock turns.

"Oh baby, right there, that's what mama likes."

He turns the volume up.

"I love you, you love me, we're a hap-py fam-i-ly…"

Bobby's eyes are fixed on the purple dinosaur, trying to block out the sounds from beyond the door.

"Look at you go, woman," the man says.

Her voice speeds up.

"Oh God, oh God, oh God."

Bobby picks up a bowl of cereal, spooning it into his mouth even though he isn't hungry. Sets it back down.

"With a great big hug…and a kiss from me to you…"

Louder.

"Won't you say you love me too?"

"That's it, get it," he yells, "come on, get it, there you go, right there."

"Smack my ass," she says.

Flesh on flesh.

"Pull my hair."

Bobby turns his head to stare at the door and tugs at his own short, brown hair.

"Harder."

He pulls again.

"Oh God," she screams.

He looks down at his pudgy hand, sticky with strands of hair.

[4.]

"How many mice do you want, Bobby? Three? Six?"

"Better give me six, he's getting so big. Eats all the time."

The pet store smells of cedar and urine, light drifting in the wall of windows at the front of the pet store, making him sweat.

"I'll say. You got enough money?"

"Got 10 dollars? Is that enough?"

"Well, they're supposed to be two bucks each, but I'll help you out here, little man."

"Thanks, Mr. Johnson. I appreciate it."

"No problem."

His back turned to the boy, the pet shop owner fishes around in the wire cage for several mice, putting them in a small cardboard box, holes punched in the sides with a rusty screwdriver.

"How's your mom doing? Haven't seen her down at Clancy's in a while. She's always a hoot. Good at darts, too."

"She's been sick. I'm taking care of her."

"Good for you, son. She need anything? I can stop by the grocery store if you want."

"Naw, we're good. It's probably just a cold or the flu or something. I give her medicine in the morning before I hop on the bus, and after school when I get home."

"You're a good son, Bobby."

Bobby hands over the mangled ten-dollar bill and takes the box in return. He peeks in the lid at the squeaking mice.

"Well, give her my best," he says.

Bobby heads out the door, a jingle of bells, and a short walk to the apartment to do his homework.

There's no snake.

[5.]

"Here you go, mom, take it down. It's not so bad."

"I hate it. It tastes bitter."

"I know, just take a swallow and then I'll bring you some tea with lemon and honey."

"My head is killing me," she says. "I can hardly sit up without everything spinning."

"Just get some rest, mom. It'll be okay.

"I'm getting sleepy again."

"It's okay, get some rest, I'll bring your tea in, set it right here beside you, so you can sip on that if you want to."

He pushes the garbage can closer to her as she lies on the couch, shaking. It's filled with tissues, crusted into little blooms of yellow and red.

"Just in case," he says.

She nods and drifts off to sleep.

Bobby returns to the kitchen and his homework, which is scattered across the table. One mouse is severed into seven pieces — head, torso, legs and tail. Blood gathers on the chopping board. The rest squeak from the box.

[6.]

"Just keep pressing harder, it's okay, I want you to," the girl says.

"But I'm worried I'll hurt you, Missy" Bobby says.

The back seat of the beige Camry is filled with a steam comprised of flowery perfume, bourbon and sweat. The windows are fogged up, blocking out the night.

"Just put your hands around my neck, push a bit more, there you go."

"Like this?"

Her voice is a whisper. Their skin is pale and shines in the dark.

"Put it back in," she says.

"Like this, Missy?"

"Oh Bobby, yes, faster."

"Like this?"

"Harder, oh yes, harder. Keep squeezing. I'll pull my own hair this time."

Her eyes start to close.

"Don't stop," she whispers.

"Oh I won't," he says, his hips moving, arms shaking as he squeezes, her body convulsing in pleasure.

"Oh, Bobby."

[7.]

"I don't know where she is," he tells the officer standing in the doorway.
"Does she do this often? Disappear?"
"All the time, Jimbo. You know that."
"And how old are you now, Bobby?"
"Robert."
"Sorry?"
"I go by Robert now."
"Since when?"
"Since I graduated, that's when."
"You going to CLC up the road?"
"Not sure yet."
"So you're 18 now, Robert?"
"Yep."
"You know a Missy Langston?"
"Sure, we dated for a bit. Why?"
"No reason. Saw her down at the arcade."
"Yeah?"
"She was saying some stuff about you."
"What do you mean?"
"She had some bruises on her neck."
"That was her idea, she's a freak."
"I heard that too, Bobby."
"Robert."
"Robert."
"What was she saying, Jimmy?"
"I don't know. Stuff. You might just want to take it easy on the rough stuff
for a while, you know? I say that as one friend to another. I'm only a couple
years older than you, and you know how people like to talk. You know these
girls, want a little attention, quick to holler rape."
"I do."

[8.]

The Camry hums, warm and dry inside. The blonde with wet stringy hair
sits in the passenger seat, a stranger, like all the rest, hands in her lap.
"Where you headed?" Robert asks.
"Just the other side of town. You going that way?"

"I am now."

The girl smiles.

"It's cold out there," she says.

"It is. I'm Robert," he says, holding out his hand.

[9.]

The small television set buzzes on the counter, filling the kitchen with static and dull light. His knife works in accordance with the voice on the set, following the directions, garbage can by his side.

"Always save the giblets. Don't waste anything. You can always use it for something.

The bones give the stew flavor, and you get every last bit of the meat this way. Just let it simmer. It'll be worth the wait, trust me."

[10.]

"You come here often?" Robert asks.

The woman looks up, bags under her eyes, her long, dark hair tangled and dull, sipping at a shot of whiskey.

"I know, such a bad line. I just mean, I haven't seen you in here before."

"Just passing through," she says.

"I'm Robert," he says, extending his hand.

HONOR

I patiently sit in the broken down bar where my mother used to whore herself. My father would beat the horny, drunk bastards to within an inch of their lives, whenever he would catch them. He always caught them, it was part of their sick little game. The bra strap that is digging into my shoulder is vying for my attention with the thong that is burrowing up my ass, so the only thing to do is down another shot of tequila and ignore the leers of my brother. Anthony. Leaning against the back wall of Nick's, the local hangout only blocks from our home, his eyes never leave me. I think he has inappropriate thoughts about me from time to time. I don't want his hands on me again, but for this one night all of the rules have been thrown out, in pursuit of fame and fortune, with a sprinkling of honor.

A flash of dishwater blond in the dull, silver mirror across from me, the fractured shelves holding all manner of tinted liquid, the hustle and bustle of people behind me, mating rituals in full swing, gambling in the shark pool, the snap of billiard balls breaking, laughter and cigarette smoke, and my parents are dead. I've worn my best cruising outfit tonight. Skin tight blue jeans hug my legs and curves, a black, lace bra that lifts and separates, a crimson silk blouse with the buttons undone to reveal ample cleavage to the boys, and pumps that say all kinds of dirty things. It's an old ritual. Spritz on some musk and bat your eyes, and a long line of eager erections will parade themselves in front of you. It's easy. But I'm married, and the third shot of tequila sits in front of me on the long wooden bar, the cool brass railing digging into my forearms. I push the picture of my doe-eyed daughter and my gentle son out of my head, they'll be starting school next week, kindergarten, and my husband lies at home in bed, crying into his pillow, unemployed for over a year now, emasculated in every way. I'm here to save us all, to earn my keep, and to appease my lecherous brother for the last time.

There are waves coursing through me and there is no desire to fight them. An electric current pulses in my nerves, the prospect of new flesh, of my hands pressed up against the cold steel bathroom stall while a strange man enters me, baring his teeth in hunger and instinct.

A dull wash of blood in my veins throbs to the beat of the jukebox at the front of the room, French doors wide open to let in cool air, the leaves outside dropping to the ground, green to mustard to copper, and I envy the pity the world has shown them, ending it all with a drifting hush. A hot splash of nausea in my stomach as the liquor sloshes around, a twinge of muscles tightening, a clenching throughout my body, fighting this alien that holds court in my center, the last bit of control slowly drifting to the edge of a cliff, balancing in a field of grass, the rocks below calling.

I look up and find the bartender watching me, his brow furrowed, lips pursed, running through the options in his head. Does he kick the drunk girl out? Does he get her another shot? Does he mind his own fucking business? I grin and close my eyes, lick my lips and let him off the hook. I tell him it's okay, I'm celebrating. I'm newly divorced, from the world it seems, but he doesn't need to know that. He smiles and pours another. It's on him this time. He understands. Just be careful he says and I nod one more time. It's time to check the room.

I spin on the green leather barstool and scan the crowd. There are rules in place here if I want to get paid. If I want to get what's mine. But if that's how it has to go down, so be it. I've sucked enough dick that it shouldn't be difficult. For three minutes of work it'll be one hell of a payday. Against all reason and will power I find myself warming up, this permission I've been given, that I've given myself. I've done worse for less.

What would mom do? Work the pool table, bending over to give the crowd a bit of her assets, while the other side of the table gets an ample amount of bosom? Probably. I'm not there yet.

Turning back around I try to summon my most desperate face. I will cry for my beer, I will make my mascara run, little black spiders leaking down my face. It isn't hard to conjure up the emotion for the task, I just think of macaroni and cheese, Dr. Seuss and the tiny little underwear with the dinosaurs on it. I hear his voice reassuring me that everything will be okay, we won't lose the house, we won't lose our retirement, our college savings, every bit of our pride. The schemes, the gambling, the disappearing for days. The begging, the pleading and the unholy love that I cannot dispel. The slap in the face that I ask for and am given.

The rough sex after the kids are asleep taking out our anger and frustration in the safest way we know, grunting and slapping flesh, bruises and bloodstained sheets, and lies to their shocked faces. Mommy had an accident. Daddy lost a scab. Nothing to be worried about and they try to believe it.

They pretend to not make any connections. But they do.

Soon I am sobbing, and the bartender at the other end, shakes his head and looks away. The girls at his end are promising and tight, eager to bare their ivory teeth, to giggle and shake their whimpering breasts. I am their future, just the other side of childbirth. I don't blame him. I'd stay down there too. His only thought is please don't vomit. And I concur.

The man at my side has appeared like a charm, concern and a soft hand resting on my shoulder, his eyes running up and down my backside even while he worries for both of us, unable to resist taking a peek down the back of my jeans. A napkin appears, and his concern is sincere, this pretty woman in distress, the easy mark, this wounded prey with the potential for acts, drunken acts that will disappear in the morning light. This is what he wants.

He is a man. Any man. Tall with two arms. He has a face and is dressed. It doesn't matter. He is the signature on the paperwork, all that I need to cross the poppy fields and enter the emerald city. The drinks come, despite my keeper's lingering look, more bright eyes and teeth, I've been rescued now. He sees that. The responsibility has been passed. A glance at Anthony, and his neck is flushed, and if he tightens his grip on that bottle of beer it'll shatter all over his lanky, damaged frame. He is a dark shadow at the edge of my vision, a cloud of gnats about my head and I swat him away and prepare for the consummation.

In a shower of golden liquid, a face ringed in salt and lime, I find myself in a familiar position, down on my knees in a foul alley behind the bar, my jeans and panties pulled down around my ankles. It has gotten out of control. It didn't have to go this far, but it has. And as my pale breasts spill out of my bra, the romeo has sprung them with his deft fingertips, tiny pink nipples pierce the air as I unzip his pants and root around for his cock.

Anthony. Always Anthony ruining my fun. A fist to the back of my dark knight's head and the unlucky rube runs his face into the brick. The laughter spills from my glossy, ruby lips. The smack of his fists are wet and overwhelming, for a moment it is sex, we are raping this poor man, and the bile is racing to the back of my throat. Enough I yell out to him, we've honored our dead. We have further built up this wall between us. Again. The windows are gone, the doorway bolted shut.

The Last Will and Testament flutters to the ground. A cheap blue Bic pen drops on top of the white. We will do it now. We have taken it far enough. I scratch out my name onto the first line, under witness. I initial it in three places, marked by tiny slivers of yellow, stray bands of streetlight pushing back to the filth. I hand it back up to this lost soul beside me. His handiwork lies in the gutter beside me, writhing in pain, adding his piss to the street. Anthony signs it, my copy splaying to the ground, a handful of doves, with broken wings. We will never see each other again. I think mom would be proud.

STEPHEN KING ATE MY BRAIN

I've been working in the plant for three months now, standing at the assembly line, scanning the conveyer belt for bent and damaged microchips. I got promoted fast, since I have a degree, and down here in Conway, Arkansas that's the way to fail up. It'll also get you into a lot of random accidents – pool cue in the gut, busted out taillights, and cigarette butts in your beer. I'm not from here; I know that much and I'm not quite sure how this happened. But I find myself in pickup trucks, most every Friday night, consoling drunk girls and filling the cab with the heady musk of sweat and orgasm. I touch the back of my head, the soft spot, the scab, and I can hear his voice, Stephen King. All I wanted to do was say hello, pick his brain a bit. Instead, I ended up here.

On the east coast there is a bookstore, a place called Bett's. They are the biggest King store in the world. I went there to meet up with some friends, fellow collectors, and to go on a tour of the town. Bangor, Maine. There was the tour of the Standpipe where he created It, books to stare at, and the massive King mansion as well. It was as I expected it. There was wrought iron with elaborate carvings of bats and crescent moons. There were brick pillars and a long yard that fell off the face of the earth. And the house…the house! Three stories high, dark and wide, crooked and pointed and dense. I stared at it long after my friends left me there. Back to the hotel room, they were cold. I couldn't take my eyes off of it, the one window on the third floor, yellow light seeping out the glass. Was it him? Was he writing the eighth book in the Dark Tower series, or the sequel to Black House? I could hear metal keys clacking, an old Remington QuietWriter, even though I knew he used a Mac. I longed to hear a wolf or coyote, a plaintive howl in the distance. I wanted the clouds to part, the full moon to fill up the night, the cold to freeze me to the spot.

Sometimes when I stand in front of the vending machine, lost in an empty, dull haze, I try to pencil in the details, what he said. I think of the expansive library, the tea, his beard. It comes to me in flashes, these bits, and I grin at the Snickers, I laugh at the Cheetos, forgetting what I wanted to eat. Forgetting I was hungry at all. I made a deal with the man, a trade, and it landed me on a bus driving out into the night.

Often my break ends and I go back to work hungry, and yet, filled with the glimmer of something he told me.

The long, black Cadillac eased up to the gate, and I stared at it, in wonder. Maybe it was a friend, or a staff member. Did he have a staff? Was it his wife or son? I knew too many personal details, I knew too much of his life. Tabitha, if you're wondering. Joe is the one with the talent. I leaned over to stare at the car, the passenger side window sliding down. The man sat inside, full beard and glasses, tired eyes filled with a shimmer.

"Better move along, son," he said. "Getting late."

"Oh, sorry, sir, I was just admiring the house. I uh, big fan, long time, I am."

He smiled.

"Sorry, I didn't think I'd see you. I've read all your books."

"Thanks," he said. "What's your name?"

"Richard. I'm a writer too, trying to break through."

"That's tough, man. But I wish you the best. You want me to sign something?"

"Um, sure. I've got a copy of The Stand here, my favorite."

"My favorite too. You sick, got a cold?"

"No," I said.

"Family history of cancer, mental illness?"

"No sir."

He looked me over, taking in the leather jacket, the jeans, my slowly expanding waistline. He licked his lips, dry from the weather, and pinched the bridge of his nose.

"Can you keep your mouth shut?" he asked.

"Uh, sure, I guess."

"No guessing. Can you keep your mouth shut?"

"Yes sir, I can."

"Hop in," he said.

Some nights when my shift is over, I sit in an old gray Taurus out in the parking lot and drink a forty ounce, no hurry to get home. Home, that's a joke. A one-bedroom apartment over a gas station, cold and sad and the only place I know. I drink it too fast, remembering words like secret and eternity and vomit the foam onto the pavement. He offered me a deal, and I took it. I had a chance to be part of his club, to be a part of the man, and to expedite my own career as well. Career, that's a joke. I can hardly remember my name, I can't add very well, and I'm not sure where I'm from. He took too much, that greedy bastard, but that's why he's the king.

We sat in his library, a low fire burning, the smell of wood smoke filling the room. We sipped at some tea—since he'd long stopped drinking—but we put it in brandy snifters for fun. He told me how he got his stories, the source of his prolific imagination. He opened a footlocker that sat by the wall, filled with manuscripts, one atop another. There must have been a dozen novels sitting in there. When I turned to him, my mouth open there was a gleam in his eye, white teeth emerging from the hairy beast that wrapped around his jaw.

He offered me a deal. I could pick any one novel out of the batch, and make it my own, for a cost. It was a guaranteed best seller, he told me more than once, and in return, just a bit of myself. He'd done this many times, he intoned, no worries, nothing to fear. Struggling young writers approached him all the time, there was no shortage of proteins to choose from. I placed the novel in my backpack, and he lay me out on his desk.

"No worries, son, I've done this lots of times."

I stared at the floor, lying on my stomach, as the needles pierced the back of my neck.

"The first one is the worst, then it's a walk in the park," he said.

Pinpricks, then the electric razor, then the scalpel. The bone saw shot a fine mist into the air, smoke from my very own skull. Something trickled down the back of my neck, and he chuckled to himself. The next smell was garlic and onions in a pan, the kitchen just off his study. My legs trembled and I feared I pissed myself, a twinge at the back of my head. My eyes rolled, fingers twitched, drool pooling under my head.

"Dammit, too much," I hear him say. "And you've pissed on my desk, you ingrate."

When I come to on the bus, the bandage wrapped around my head, the throbbing in my skull pushing tears out of my eyes, I am nowhere near Maine. The slow vibration of tires underneath me has woken me up. I'm in the middle of the darkness, cornfields and billboards on a bus ride heading someplace south. My backpack is filled with tightly wrapped cash, in bundles of twenties and tens. But no novel, no book. There is only a note. It apologies for ruining me like this, but I'll be unable to tour, to promote, and quite possibly in time, to tie my shoes.

It could all go away at any time, he writes, his apologies for the slip. Get a simple job in a small town and just whittle away the time.

He suggests coke and whores and cheap beer, and in the end, I take him up on it all.

Some days when I stand in line at McDonald's, or at the video store, I get a flash of his bearded face. He tells me of all of the brains he has eaten, just a nip, just a slice, just a bite. And I smile. I could never really write anyway. It's probably better this way.

TWENTY REASONS TO STAY
AND ONE TO LEAVE

Because in the beginning it was the right thing to do, staying with her, comforting and holding her, while inside I was cold and numb, everything on the surface an act, just for her.

Because I couldn't go outside, trapped in the empty expanse of rooms that made me twitch, echoes of his voice under the eaves, and in the rafters.

Because she still hid razorblades all over the house.

Because I wasn't ready to bare myself to the world, willing to pour more salt into the wounds.

Because of the dolls and the way she held them to her bare breasts, the way she laughed and carried on, two dull orbs filling her sockets, lipstick on her face, hair done up, but the rest of her like marble, to go with her porcelain children that watched from his bed, defiling it, making a joke of it all.

Because at one point in our past she saved me from myself, the simple act of showing up. Lasagna filled my apartment with garlic and promise when all I could do was fall into a bottle.

Because I kept hoping he would walk in the door, backpack flung over his shoulder, eager to show me his homework, the worlds he had created with a handful of crayons.

Because it was my fault, the accident, and we both knew it.

Because if she was going to die a death of a thousand cuts, one of them wouldn't be mine.

Because tripping over a Matchbox car, I found myself hours later curled up in a ball, muttering and listening for his response.

Because she asked me to, and I hadn't learned to say no to her yet.

Because she wanted to live in any time but this time, jumping from one era to another, bonnets and hoop skirts, wigs and parasols, and I allowed it.

Because when I held her in the black void that was our bedroom, pressing my body up against hers, part of me believed I was a sponge, soaking up her pain. It was a fake voodoo, but it was all that I had.

Because I had no love left for anyone in the world.

Because I didn't want to go.

Because it was still my home, and not simply a house yet.

Because I wasn't done talking to my son, asking him for forgiveness.

Because I didn't believe that we were done, that our love had withered, collapsed and fallen into his casket, wrapping around his broken bones, covering his empty eyes.

Because I didn't hate her enough to leave.

Because I didn't love her enough to leave.

Because every time she looked at me, she saw him, our son, that generous boy, and it was another gut punch bending her over, another parting of her flesh, and I was one of the thousand, and my gift to her now was my echo.

TRANSMOGRIFY

In order to live I have to die.

I close my eyes for a second and her hot mouth is on my nipples, her hands cupping my breasts as our pale limbs writhe on the bed. A shock of air and my eyes flick open. I run my tongue over porcelain teeth, breathing in the crisp November air, and exhaling strawberry frost. Still, the remorse. When will I learn?

Numb to the bone I stand in the empty graveyard as the sun creeps over the horizon, limping home, drenched in a bloodmist that constantly frames my vision. The acid-rain will soon eat through the screeners I've put on. At this time of year AR50 may not be enough. As much as things have changed some traditions stay the same. I come back to the rituals. The burial.

In the distance leaves burn, wet and moldy. A dense cloud of dirty smoke drifts over the skeletal forest that rings the iron fence, chipped and forgotten. I am alone, as expected. The obituary was a formality but I'm a stickler for details. Long slender fingers push deep into the cashmere overcoat abyss that drapes to my knees and hugs my empty shell. The sharp wind rapes me again and again. I play a game in the flayed tresses that flit about my face. They are as black as my heart and I hide from the very surroundings I set out to embrace today.

Footsteps. I glance around, picking up the motion of a lone figure, head down, treading towards me. Dark and tall, it must be Remy. Who else would show? Who else was left? I shiver but not from the cold. I fed last night and am still full of the sustenance of her lifeforce. She had been expecting something akin to a gothic romance but was sorely mistaken.

The evolution didn't happen all at once. It took time. Years. Lifetimes. But

I have plenty of time. I have eternity.

I rub the port at the base of my skull, a nasty habit like twirling my hair. I have to see DocAught soon. Time for a tune-up. A little nanotech and a full viral upgrade and nobody will be the wiser.

A thousand voices whisper and my eyes shoot to the dead branches. A Starling catapults up into the fading light, fluttering its wings. Panic stricken eyes gaze my way as it drops from the sky, twitching for but a moment, then still. Rigid.

He is closer now. There is nowhere to run. Not that I could have. I miss him. When he finally looks up his eyes go wide and his brow furrows, stopping in his tracks. A heat flushes my skin and for a moment I hesitate. The longing blurs my vision as the heat flows to a million points of skin that weep beneath my clothes.

"Excuse me, miss," he says.

"You must be Remy," I say.

"Um...well, yes, but..." his eyes are on my face like a magnifying glass - inspecting, doubting.

"I'm Cinder. But you can call me Cindy," I offer.

"OH, right. Wow. Finally we meet. It's just..."

"I know. I look just like her."

"Well, twenty years ago, right...the same blue eyes, uncanny."

"Consider it an homage. I had them dyed to the same Tiffany blue a couple of years ago. Mine had always been such a boring brown."

"Right." He turns to the grave and stares at the headstone. "Old school."

"It's mostly symbolic, you know, with the organ laws and all..."

"Yes. She's not in there. I know."

"You ok, Remy?"

"I didn't think there'd be anybody here, especially not you. I thought you were a myth, something that she talked about at night, a phantom that didn't really exist."

"Long story. Nothing you need to know about. Pedestrian."

"Right."

"I was just leaving anyway, it's getting late. Curfew."

"Yes." He stands close to me, a massive presence, more grey at the temples than I remember.

"Here, Remy, she wanted me to give you this."

I walk over to him, every bit of silk rubbing against my flesh, screaming out. I wrap my arms around him and press my head against his chest.

The pounding. His hands are on my back and I find myself turning feline. I purr into his grey woolen coat and rub my face in his musky scent. Wormwood and formaldehyde burn my nostrils as I brush up against his legs. My knees are like a cricket making music as they rub together.

For a second he lets down his guard. Remorse and anguish float to the surface like a bloated corpse wrapped in black trash bags.

Against my own wishes I take a sip. Just a bit of him for posterity. A quick inhale and he coughs. I lick my lips, rubbing out a bitter coat of wax that I'd pasted on earlier. Ruby Woo. The casing is new, but the inhabitant, ancient.

I push away and step back. For a moment we are knee deep in snow, the Celtic crosses and cracked stones dusted with powder, as his breath exhales in a cloud, eyes dimming to dull ashes. He staggers, barely able to raise his hands from his sides. A crack over the horizon as the sound barrier breaks. The 6:42 to Los Angeles. Always on time.

"It's ok, baby. Everything is going to be fine."

Remy falls over on his side, glancing up at me, his eyes empty.

"You won't remember this moment, for I've taken it. Forget me. Forget her. We're gone, and won't be back. It's better this way. Consider it a bullet dodged Remy and move on with your life. Let it go."

"Ok."

"Down the street from you, that blonde with the synthetics, the skin job on a leash she calls a dog, that one. She's a good catch for you. Don't come here again."

"Ok."

I need to go home and jack in. Now. My hunger has been awakened. He'll be ok. He'll be alive. It's the least I can do for him after all of these years. Samantha is dead now. Long live Cinder. Half of the time I'm gone anyway. It doesn't matter.

I'll always be alone.

Standing at the grocery checkout the young girl with the blonde ponytail can't look at me enough. Her face flushes red every fifteen seconds. She scans the bizarre selections that I've grabbed in a frenzy as the ache washes over me in waves. Six blood oranges. A 24 oz. bottle of Intrigue K-Y Gelly. 1 gallon of compressed nitrogen.

"Are you, like...I mean, do I..." she sputters.

"No."

"Oh, ok."

12 razor blades. A six-pack of Frost Gatorade. 8 cellular protein cutlets.

"Are you sure? I mean, didn't I see..."

"No, sweetheart, you didn't."

12 feet of Tripp Lite U042-036 High-Speed USB 2.0 cable. A tube of black cherry lip balm. A 6.8 oz. Red Currant Votivo candle. A 50-count bottle of Vitamin B12-H_SharkOil.

"I mean, I don't like girls or anything, that's not what I'm trying..."

"Honey, look at me."

The high school cheerleader with the punk rock fantasies pauses for a moment with a can of Vienna Sausages in her left hand, the other wandering up to her shirt collar, fiddling with the tab, running behind her neck to massage the only acceptable exposed flesh.

A flash of light and French doors fly open. An empty bed rests in the middle of the room as pale blue moonlight fills the space with stardust. A cigarette smolders in an ashtray on the nightstand as the dull patter of a shower running seeps from beneath the bathroom door. There is an indentation in the mattress. Lace trim edges the sheets, wrinkled ivory bunched in piles. It is quiet in the room but for the echo of a gasp, the exhale of air, and the sigh of completion.

"You couldn't handle it..." squinting at her name tag, "...Jennifer."

I extend my wrist to the scanner, and run the bar-code over it. BEEP. Cinder Bathory. $426,384. Transaction ok? $1,235.45. Accessing account. APPROVED.

Welcome to Facebook. Facebook helps you connect and share with the entities in your life.

I try to pry the plastic off of the new USB cable. These damn things are so hard to open. My hair is pulled back and to the side for easy access to my port. My skin is pink and splotchy from the blistering hot shower and the obsidian silk robe clings to my damp body like tape.

My hands shake and drop the package to the floor. The third one I've burnt out this month. Nothing has any depth anymore, nothing satisfies. Everything is manufactured, and that makes it farther from the truth, the core of it all, the purity. Soon the snacking will not be enough.

I pause for a second to gaze around my sparse studio apartment.

I live like an eccentric millionaire, eating cans of cat food and fearing my own demise while my checking account stands at $400,000. There is nothing but Glacier water and a hexagrid of hemaglobin cubes in the fridge. The grocery bag stands on the counter forgotten for the moment. A king size four-post bed covered with 1000-thread count sheets fills the room. It was hand carved by Buddhist monks four thousand years ago. A blinking 36" monitor sits next to a hybrid computer that I found in Chinatown. Resting on the beaten Salvation Army desk, it waits for me, the leather desk chair eager for my supplication.

It has Intel guts, Mac OS XX_Cheetah, a terabyte of hard drive space, and enough security to route whatever happens back to the very brown coats that might be tracking me.

I should move to the desert and leave it all. I've evolved beyond my needs, and my life is more complicated for it. The itching of the nanodrones is in my head, DocAught says. It isn't possible for me to feel them. But I do.

They crash around the inside of my veins and the siren songs, the rapture, makes me double over and crash to my knees. I tear open the plastic, slicing my index finger in the process. By the dull glow of the monitor I suck at the broken skin, as my eyes slide into whiteness. My history will be my undoing, but it is not the crimson shot I want tonight. They wait for me, a bunch of addicts, scratching at the scabs, ready to tear them open again. And I'm coming. I'm coming.

I unravel the cord and jam it into the side of the computer. Sliding into the small leatherbound swivel chair I fumble around at the base of my skull and plug it in. My eyes flutter and a gasp escapes my lips. Fingers fly to the keyboard as I login. I have 432 friends. I have 23 new messages. I've been poked 12 times. I skip it all and head to a special private chat room. There are others like me. Others that think they are like me. But they aren't.

Tomorrow they'll be weak, fatigued, with headaches or migraines, depressed over something they can't quite figure out. Their immune systems will plummet and regardless of the hyperdermics they shove into their thighs or the bots they have infiltrating their systems, my tech is better. They plug in just like I do, seeking something to fill the void.

PRIVATE CHAT - Room 2112.0101
Bloodrunners
[2] members present
Ashestoashes has entered the room

cureforpain: hey ash, wassup

breakingthebroken: so i didn't think that was fair, you know?

cureforpain: nk, lb

breakingthebroken: sistersister, where have you been?

ashestoashes: oh you know, same old stuff, stupid job, stupid boyfriend, blech

breakingthebroken: we were just talking about that crap

cureforpain: ask her, she'll tell you

ashestoashes: what?

breakingthebroken: oh, nothing, stupid boy i think is working me

ashestoashes: what do you mean?

breakingthebroken: i'm just being paranoid that's all

ashestoashes: what happened

cureforpain: come on, spill it or i will

ashestoashes: you can tell me

breakingthebroken: <sigh> i text him, and it's always real fast and short, brb, or he won't take my calls, and when i ask him what he's doing he never tells me, i try to hook up, and can't find him, you know, stupid shit but then...

I lean back in the chair and close my eyes. The flow is slow but unmistakable. Fear, bits of anxiety, regret, remorse. Even Cureforpain is letting it out. He's been trying to get Broken in the real world for months now. Anger, frustration.

ashestoashes: let just tell you something, and you just listen, ok?

breakingthebroken: ok

cureforpain: here it comes, preach baby :-)

ashestoashes: if he never returns your calls, if he never has sex with you, if he blows you off for his boys, if he's always working late, never wants to see the movies you do, never wants to eat the food you like, basically, he just doesn't care about you, move on...

The rig has been filled and the air tapped out. Leaning forward I'm blinded by a shroud of white as memories cut in and out. Mountains and a cabin, AUF WIEDERSEHEN! gunfire and the pounding of horses hooves thundering by. The cold stone of an empty hallway lost deep in the bowels of some ancient castle. Snow and the soft rub of animal fur on my naked flesh.

My fingers fly over the keyboard, lecturing the kids once again.

...if he won't let you look at his phone sadness, frustration, anger, betrayal that means there are calls on there or texts he doesn't want you to see, numbers, and if his phone rings fury, despair, failure, remorse, exhaustion, nausea at his apartment and the voicemail starts to pick up and you hear a female voice, and he purrs in your ear, hold on a sec baby abandonment, suicide, desperation, failure, anger, anger, anger, stupidity, loss while he jumps up to answer it and you hear the words nothing or nobody or later, then he is screwing you over he is using you loneliness, rage, fury, emptiness, anxiety...

> breakingthebroken: omg i'm gonna barf
> breakingthebroken has left the room
> ashestoashes: too much?
> cureforpain: naw, she needed to hear it
> ashestoashes: so what's up with you?

The sun peeks under the edge of the velvet drapes. Exhausted, I breathe in and out, my skin heating up, tightening.

I've turned back the clock three years tonight. I'm five pounds lighter. Sweat glistens on my exposed throat, and I lean back in the chair as my hand slides down the front of my robe. My eyes close as I embrace this mortal coil.

There are predators and there are prey. Donors and recipients.

I have to move around a lot. I have a Xenon AmTran card. I have five million frequent flier miles. Conway, Arkansas. Rolla, Missouri. Peoria, Illinois. Off the beaten path. The security is too dangerous in the metropolitan factions. You can only nibble on the second shift of the Dell computer parts factory for so long. The Caterpillar assembly line. The AT&TGlobal telemarketing center. They start to get sick. People stop showing up, and glances dart my way. They think it's sex. When the whispers at the vending machines start, it's time for me to disappear into the night.

The places where emotions are raw and on the surface, that's where I linger. But in time I find that no matter how depressing the job, how dismal the future, how anxious my friends become, it has its limits. People leave, people get a bad vibe about you, and they stop opening up. The funeral homes call the police. The hospitals ask for ID. The AA meetings start questioning your steps. Their hackles go up, and their senses heighten. Online it's easier to sip. And the body of water that I surf with reckless abandon is much larger and better stocked.

I'm tired of writing pablum for the broken hearted wrist slashing nation. I need to reinvent myself. I need a new home.

DocAught is coming tonight. A house call. Like he does every hundred years or so. Something has to go in the casket where Samantha should be. They may harvest every organ for the good of the people, every bloodshot eyeball and broken digit. But there is always something left. You'd be surprised how many useless parts we have. The vomeronasal organ, a tiny pit on each side of the septum. A set of cervical ribs left over from our reptilian days. The male uterus. A fifth toe. It isn't pretty.

I need to get ready, prepare myself for the transition.

Silence has expanded to fill my tiny apartment. A section of candlelight throbs from the window ledge. A pair of forlorn window frames blast the studio with a foul chill.

I am rotting from the inside out and have waited much too long. The door hangs open wide, a forlorn shriek that swallows the light. I will not be disturbed for this space does not exist. Not tonight.

My pasty skin is a moonglow in the center of a collapsing star. Eyes closed, my face is buried in the lavender scent of the downy pillows. A thin sheen of icy sweat coats my body as my soul fights to escape. Any other night and my head would be filled with visions of fingertips and razor blades, bloodletting and rope burns, tongues shoved into every eager crevice. There is no room for that tonight. Shoulders twitch, my hands grasping and releasing the bedsheets, and I repeat one word over and over again.

Transmogrify.

I have lost myself again. Torches burn at the river's edge. There is the sharp snapping of canine teeth and the grumbling of angry peasants.

"No...no."

Convulsions and my neck snaps back, eyes rolling up into my skull, my tongue darting for moisture in every corner of my mouth.

Forward, back. Forward, back. Flying sideways, a hard turn to the right, pulled around a corner, and gravity pulls my stomach down, pressure on my face, a great rush of wind.

He's here.

I don't need to see him to picture him clearly. So many times we've done this. My keeper. So many times we've hunted together. My lover. His hand is on my bare back, the size of a stingray. His weight crushes the bed and it cries out in resistance. Not a sound from him, not a word. I can't remember the last thing he said to me. Yes. Yes, I can.

"Go."

A tingle races over the surface of my skin as he runs his massive paw up the small of my back, stopping just short of my port. A sigh escapes my lips as a solitary bloody tear glides down my cheek.

I picture him the way I last saw him, in a back alley of New York City, 1908. A bowler hat atop his bald, gleaming dome. The dark wool suit stretched taut across his broad shoulders, his legs like tree stumps ending in squared off shoes. His prominent nose crowding out small, gleaming eyes, a fire burning inside, his full lips tight. The clink of a beer glass dropped on cobblestone, and his patience had run out. Just like that.

He leans over me and presses his body against mine, his cold musculature like a marble sculpture. I am slowly being suffocated by a distant god and I don't care. A harp string vibrates and the clasp of a briefcase opens. Plastic unwraps and latex gloves snap on.

The slow turning of a lid being removed fills my ears as a hint of birch mixed with sassafras drifts to me.

I am waiting for the cord, the cable, the life. He is not.

One hand is firm at the base of my neck and a device is shoved in the port. A leap drive. I struggle but cannot move. He holds me down with one giant palm as the toxic potion fills my nostrils, burning, and the drive comes to life with a hum.

"There are creatures far worse than you, my love," his baritone rumbles.

I am emptying, spilling, falling from a great height as my eyes gush a river. A soul I thought to be long gone, diseased and broken, breaks. Not a single utterance, only the spinning and whirring of the pod at my neck. Outside my window in the suicide of winter there is a void of life. A crackling of ice as a solitary branch fractures under the weight and shatters on the ground.

RUDY JENKINS BURIES HIS FEARS

Realizing that his mom and dad were never going to believe him, Rudy equipped himself for the long night ahead: the heavy butcher's knife sharpened to a glean, a handful of garlic bulbs stuffed under his pillow, the 1964 JFK silver dollar that his grandmother had given him in her will. He was taking no chances.

It was late summer, but he'd been wearing long sleeved shirts to school for weeks now, to cover his arms. The bite marks, the cuts, the mottled bruises that ran up and down his back, there was no explaining it to his friends, the teachers. They saw a ten-year-old boy that played too rough, and his parents didn't see the marks at all. He held out his arms in front of his mother, while he stood there shivering, waiting for the towel, but she hardly saw him at all. His skinny pale frame dripping with water was no match for her intent gaze in the mirror, the puffy dark circles under her eyes, her right hand constantly kneading something: her long neck, aching back, and trembling hands.

In the beginning there were growls, long hair brushing across his face, and the stench of something rotten. But he wouldn't open his eyes. No matter what happened, his eyes stayed shut. The beast sat at the end of his bed, its hulking shadow cast out into the night, blanketing the wall with an expansive permanence.

And in the morning, the window was always left open a crack to let in fresh air, the faint scent of his mother's lilac bushes a reminder that he was still alive, the sound of a garbage truck rumbling to a halt, slamming plastic cans back to the ground, a lifetime away. His sheets were usually stained with blood, scratches up and down his arms healing into scabs, his translucent white underpants sticking to his flesh.

He'd learned to do his own laundry, Shout a lost voice yelled into the washing machine, bleach stinging his nose, making his eyes water. He often stood there and bawled.

But this night, it would be different. He arranged a half circle of pebbles just inside his door, perfectly smooth grey and brown rocks that he hunted for on his walk home from school. A basket of dried sage withered in an abalone shell that he placed in the northeast corner of his room. He bent over it reciting words and prayers that he hardly understood, stolen from the internet while his parents watched tv. In the name of the father it sat smoldering, a wisp of dying smoke lifting into the air.

When it came for him, he was ready, and yet, he still felt a trickle of urine run down the inside of his thigh. Its meaty paws ran over the covers, patting him down, squeezing his flesh, testing him for the meal that was inevitable. Rudy shivered under the blankets, layers and layers of blankets, still cold, and still sweating. His eyes were clenched shut as hard as he could squeeze them until stars shattered the dark underbelly of his eyelids, filling his head with a supernova of distress.

And then a slap of cold air, the blankets ripped off, and the foul stench leaked out of its gaping maw, drifting to him on a wave of buzzing flies. Its breathing labored, stuttering with excitement.

When its full weight pushed down on the bed, sitting right beside him, he shot out his shaking hand, filled with the angry blade, jabbing and jabbing, meeting flesh, parting it, his own whimpering mixing with the grunts of the wounded animal. And the weight lifted. It lumbered and tripped, and was gone. Rudy's eyes remained closed. A rivulet of sticky fluid ran down his hand and over the downy hair of his arm.

In the morning, his room was filled with the heavy scent of sage, the window still closed, a scattering of rocks by his open door. He carried the bloody sheets out to the back yard, easing past the sounds of percolating coffee and frying pans banging on the stove, out into the wet grass, jaw tight with determination. The rusty shovel leaned against the side of the house. With shoelaces leaking over the edge of the blade he pushed it into the soft soil, hands twitching with memory, turning over new earth. The hole would now be filled with these baptized fibers, one void traded for another, one space filled, as another. He crossed himself and went back inside.

Blinking his eyes, hastily dressed for school, Rudy sat at the table, his mother a blur, everything moving so fast. He kept his head low so as not to disturb the holy grace that had entered the house, gone for so long. He bowed over his plate of runny eggs, trying to find enough air in the room, the snap of his father's newspaper making him jump again and again.